# SURVIVAL

*We shall draw from the heart of suffering itself the means of inspiration and survival.'*

*Winston Churchill*

*'Our pleasures were simple - they included survival.'*

*Dwight D. Eisenhower*

# By

# G.S.Willmott

# Acknowledgements

Thank you to Anna my wife for continuing to tolerate my obsession
Thank you to the three preview readers:
Ian Jones
Christine McIntyre
David Crooks
Thank you Desma Paccito for another great book cover
Thank you Sheelagh Wegman for a great edit

# Contents

# 1. Disaster

## 15<sup>th</sup> April 1912

The American Navy officer was dining at the captain's table with his wife and children. They were enjoying their main course; Lucy and the two children were having lamb with mint sauce while Joe was enjoying Roast Sirloin of Beef Forestière.

> 'Captain Doherty, would you care to join me on the bridge? The equipment we have installed is state-of-the-art. I think you will enjoy the experience.

> 'Certainly Captain Smith. I would be honoured, Sir.'

> 'Will you and the children be okay darling? I will meet you back in our cabin.'

> 'You go ahead Joe, we'll be fine. Enjoy yourself - you will be in your element.'

Captain Joe Doherty followed Captain Smith up to the ship's bridge. It certainly was impressive.

**The *Titanic*'s Bridge**

Captain Doherty counted six officers on the bridge; performing various duties, they all seemed pretty busy.

The observer in the crow's nest, Able Seaman Fleet, spotted a gigantic iceberg dead ahead. The time was 11.40 pm. Fleet instantly rang the six-inch brass bell in the crow's nest three times and lifted the telephone to the bridge.

Sixth Officer James Moody answered.

Fleet's message was chillingly brief: 'Iceberg dead ahead.'

'Thank you,' replied Moody.

Captain Smith and his American guest were enjoying a cognac in the Captain's sitting room. They were unaware of the drama-taking place on the bridge.

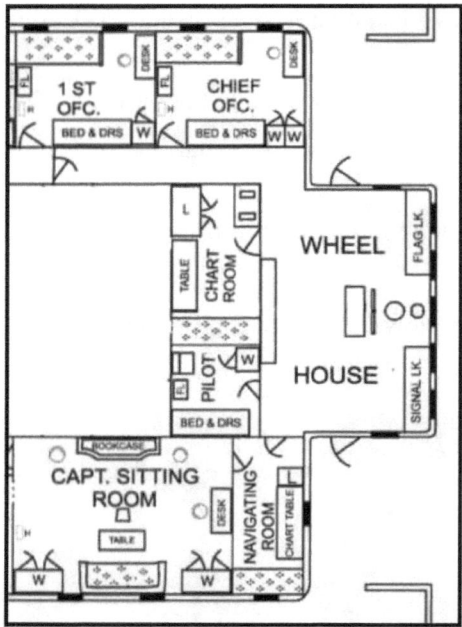

Fleet could see the iceberg looming nearer by the second. On the bridge, William Murdoch, the ship's First Officer, responded to the message from the crow's nest by giving the order, 'Hard a-starboard.'

This meant that the ship's bow would swing to port. At the same time, he gave an order to the engine room, 'Stop. Full speed astern.' Acting swiftly, he also pushed a bell-button for ten seconds to warn those below that he intended to close all the watertight doors. He then pulled the switch that automatically closed them. It was too late- evidence suggested that Fleet had spotted the iceberg at a distance of less than five hundred yards, and unfortunately, the *Titanic* took over eight hundred yards to stop at that speed.

Murdoch's actions caused the *Titanic* to avoid a head-on collision, and nearly the entire iceberg; however, there was only enough time to turn the ship two points, which resulted in a devastating blow. As it transpired, this was the worst possible scenario. As it moved along the side of the ship, the iceberg scraped along the first three hundred feet of the hull. As it passed amidships, Murdoch ordered the helm hard to port in order to clear the stern. The berg passed beyond the stern and drifted silently away into the distance.

Captain Smith had been warned of icebergs only hours before and he and Captain Doherty raced out to the bridge, but it was all too late, the *Titanic* had started to sink quickly.

Joe excused himself and quickly proceeded to his family's cabin but it was extremely difficult because most of the passengers were running in the opposite direction. Finally he reached his cabin and found it was vacant.

'That's good,' he thought, 'they must have headed up to the lifeboats.'

Just then the ship's stern lifted up forty feet and Joe started to slide down the passageway as if it was a slippery slide. He tried to grab the handrail but the highly polished brass made it impossible to grip. Cabin doors were swinging wildly. Joe was struck in the temple, rendering him unconscious. He slid into the black oily water engulfing the ship.

Lucy and the children had made their way to the top deck where the lifeboats were located. They were in one of the first boats lowered into the cold North Atlantic. They were certainly not dressed for the evacuation; Lucy was wearing an evening gown and the children were in their night attire.

The lifeboat was floating on an icy sea on a cold moonless light. The other lifeboats were scattered around the area with everyone trying to keep warm and keeping a lookout for other passengers. At 2:15 am, with fifteen hundred people still aboard, the *Titanic* began to go under. As the bow plunged beneath the waves, Jack Phillips and Harold Bride sent out the last wireless call for help. A minute later, the ship's lights flickered and went out. The only lights available to guide survivors were from the stars. As the remaining passengers and crew clung desperately to the deck rails, the stern of the *Titanic* rose higher into the air and stood vertically for about 30 seconds.

At 2:20 am, the *Titanic* snapped between the third and fourth funnels and the stern dipped down and hit the water as the bow plunged to the bottom of the sea. As the stern filled with water it rose slightly into the air and began to spin. It then quickly disappeared beneath the surface of the water and began its long descent two a half miles to the ocean floor.

The remaining fifteen hundred passengers went down with the ship. Captain Joe Doherty was one of them.

Screams and cries filled the air, as the remaining passengers floated in the freezing water. The cries continued haunting the survivors in the lifeboats. Only a few lifeboats wanted to go back for more people. Most of them thought they would get 'swamped' if they went back. After a while, the cries died down and there came a deadly silence.

At 3:30 am, rockets were sighted. These were from the rescue ship, the *Carpathia*. The first lifeboat was picked up at 4:10 am and the last was picked up at 8:30 am. At 8:50 am, the *Carpathia* headed for New York, arriving there on April 18 at 9:00 pm. She carried seven hundred and five survivors. Lucy, Jack and Julie Doherty were among them.

***Carpathia* Rescue Boats**

What were this ambitious young US Navy Captain and his family doing on the ill-fated *Titanic*?

# 2.  Disappointment

## Washington DC 1910

Captain Joe Doherty was walking beside the Anacostia River on his way to an important meeting. The river wound through Washington and although not as significant as the Potomac River it played a significant part in the life of Washington DC

The walk would take him to the Washington Naval Yard where he had been summoned to meet with Rear-Admiral Eugene Leutze. Joe was hoping the meeting would confirm a commission for one of the latest New York class battleships. Commanding a ship of this magnitude had been his ambition since he joined the Navy at the age of seventeen. He would often dream of being on the bridge orchestrating manoeuvres during one of the great naval battles. Joe had been raised in the Chesapeake Bay area where he had enjoyed a privileged childhood attending the Severn School; the prep school for the United States Naval Academy. His sister, Anna, and he played in the leafy street without fear of predators. Joe wasn't the brightest kid in the school; that honour went to Anna but he wasn't far off it. After graduation he had no trouble being accepted into the Naval Academy. His father had graduated twenty-five years before and had commanded several battleships. Joe had some large shoes to fill.

His time at the Academy went without incident and he graduated in 1900 as an Ensign and was assigned to the *New Hampshire* a Connecticut Class Battleship.

**The *New Hampshire* in New York**

Now the moment of truth had arrived. He waited in the Admiral's anteroom with a fair amount of trepidation. At last he was summoned into the spacious office where his old friend greeted him.

'Hello Joe, it's good to see you. How is that lovely wife of yours?'

'She's well thanks, Admiral.'

'Please Joe, we go back a long way. Call me Gene while we are alone in this office.'

'Of course Gene. I am sorry.'

'Don't be sorry Joe - just less formal.'

'How are the children? Growing up I would imagine?'

'All too quickly for my liking, Gene.'

'How old are they now?'

'Jack is sixteen and Julie is fourteen.'

'My boy Theo is fourteen going on twenty one. Well Joe, I suppose we should get on with business. I know you would like nothing more than to command a battleship and you will, but not for now.'

Joe looked perplexed and his heart sank.

'I need you to perform a key role for me. As you are aware the Germans are building up their battle fleet at an alarming rate. The British are still way in front and have increased their shipbuilding to maintain their naval superiority. We, as you are aware, are also increasing our fleet, though not as fast as these two European powers.

'I am sending you to London as our new Naval Attaché to represent our strategic interests and report back to me on what the English and Germans are up to. The assignment is for two years and when you return I promise you will command the best and most modern ship in our fleet.'

'When am I required to leave, Gene?'

'In four weeks, on the 1st of March.'

'Well, I would be lying if I said I was thrilled. But I know you wouldn't send me if it wasn't important.'

'Just remember Joe – in two years you will have the best job in the Navy.'

The two officers shook hands. Joe took the same route back to his office, pausing to sit on a park bench trying to reconcile his immediate future.

He arrived home at about six o'clock and poured himself a Scotch, and a gin and tonic for his wife Lucy.

'So, how was your day, Darling? You look like you had a tough one.'

'I didn't get the commission I was hoping for. Or not yet anyway.'

'Oh, I am sorry. Why?'

'We are going to London for two years. You are looking at the new Naval Attaché.'

There was plenty to organise prior to their departure, not least the children's schooling. At least they had a house in Richmond Park to move into provided by the Navy. The Embassy helped organise the right schools for the children - Julie was enrolled in the North London Collegiate School while Jack would attend Harrow.

# 3.  The Bright Lights of London

The 1<sup>st</sup> March arrived and the family boarded the RMS *Olympia* for the six-day voyage departing from New York.

The family enjoyed the first class voyage, the parents relaxing in the lounge while the children played with the new friends they had made.

The *Olympia* was regarded as the finest passenger ship afloat; consequently the voyage went without incident and the ship berthed at London Docks on 7th March.

Joe, his wife and children were greeted by a Lieutenant attached to the Embassy and after they passed through immigration and customs they were driven to their new home in Richmond Park. London intrigued them all; they passed Buckingham Palace and saw Big Ben in the distance. All these sights would become very familiar to them over the coming two years.

The Dohertys soon settled into the London way of life, visiting London monuments and the many museums and art galleries dominated the first three months.

Joe also settled into his new role as Naval Attaché meeting his British, French and German counterparts. It became obvious to him that the European major powers were ramping up their arsenals. He submitted a report to Washington once a month.

May 1st 1910

Confidential Report to Rear Admiral Eugene Leutze

Dear Sir,

It has become very clear that the British and German navies are competing in a significant navy arms race.

The British, as you are aware, have recently launched the Dreadnought class Battleship.

HMS *Dreadnought*: 17,900 tons; 526 feet in length; ten 12 inch guns, eighteen 4 inch guns, five torpedo tubes; maximum belt armour 11 inches; top speed 21.6 knots.

I was able to take this photo recently.

My intelligence tells me they intend to build eight more Dreadnoughts over the next two years. The German navy is trying to match the British firepower by building their own Dreadnought class Battleships.

Both countries seem to be following the theory of Alfred Mayan: He who controls the oceans controls the world.

I have established the relative numbers to date by both sides.

Dreadnoughts Launched

|  | Great Britain | Germany |
|---|---|---|
| 1906 | 1 | 0 |
| 1907 | 3 | 0 |
| 1908 | 2 | 4 |
| 1909 | 2 | 3 |
| 1910 | 3 | 1 |
| TOTAL | 11 | 8 |

Dreadnought Battle Cruisers

|  | Great Britain | Germany |
|---|---|---|
| 1906 | 0 | 0 |
| 1907 | 3 | 0 |
| 1908 | 0 | 0 |
| 1909 | 1 | 0 |
| 1910 | 1 | 2 |
| TOTAL | 5 | 2 |

I believe these numbers will increase substantially over the next few years.

This battleship race will obviously impact our own construction plans. I await your instructions.

Yours truly,

Captain Joseph Doherty

Lucy had settled into the London way of life although all her friends were American. They would meet for tea once a week and played Gin Rummy every

Friday. She was rather hoping she would meet some nice English ladies but had not really had the opportunity to establish friendships as yet. Jack and Julie had settled into their new schools - Jack was even playing cricket, a sport he had never heard of, let alone played before.

The house the Government provided was a three-story terrace, which kept everybody fit with continually going up and down the stairs.

One Thursday morning Lucy went out to the letterbox to see if they had received any mail, not that they received much, just the odd letter from home and a few bills.

She noticed a letter with the British Royal Family crest and hurried back inside and opened the envelope.

*BY THE KING'S COMMAND*

*A Reception*

*Will be held by*

*HIS ROYAL HIGHNESS KING GEORGE*

*And*

*The Queen Consort*

*In the garden of Buckingham Palace*

*Wednesday, 29th July 1911, from 4 p.m. to 6 p.m.*

*Admit Captain Joseph Doherty and Mrs L Doherty*

*At the Grand Entrance, at the Grosvenor Gardens Gate, or the Constitution Hill Gate.*

Lucy could not believe her eyes - they were going to meet the King and Queen of England! They were going to Buckingham Palace, the magnificent palace they drove past almost every day.

The time was four o'clock; Joe would be home at six. She would have to contain her excitement until he got home from the Embassy.

The time went slowly as she tried to busy herself, getting the evening meal together and doing some ironing. The children couldn't understand their mother's mood but she decided Joe should be informed first, then Jack and Julie. At last she heard the Embassy car drop off her husband. He opened the front door to find Lucy in a great state of excitement.

'What's going on, Darling?'

'Joe, we have received an invitation to a Royal Garden Party at Buckingham Palace. We are going to meet the King and Queen … can you imagine?'

'Darling that's wonderful, but I don't think you should get your hopes up too high. There will probably be a couple of hundred people there with similar aspirations to us.'

'I don't care! The fact that we are invited is something very special, and you never know - we may meet the monarchs. I have to start thinking about what I should wear. Of course I'll have to buy a new outfit. You'll be okay I expect, you will be wearing your uniform.'

Joe just listened and agreed with his very excited wife.

'This will do her the world of good,' he thought.

He had heard from Admiral Leutze that day and that's what preoccupied his thoughts. Joe retired into his study with a glass of single malt and thought about the Admiral's directive.

He accepted Joe's report as accurate and unbiased; he now wanted Joe to clandestinely determine all troop and weapons build-up of all the major powers, including Russia. The President was concerned that a major war was not far away.

Joe had been allocated a significant budget to pay officers of all sides to divulge state secrets. He had never thought of himself as a spy but that's what he had been ordered to become.

# 4. I Spy

William Taft was the President of the United States from 1909 until 1913 and had been Secretary of War from 1904 to 1908. He therefore had a keen interest in what was happening in Europe and the sabre rattling that seemed to be happening. His main concerns centred on the treaties that had been signed between various European powers and also some Asian countries such as Japan.

July 1st 1910


Confidential Report to Rear Admiral Eugene Leutze


Dear Sir,

I have begun to accumulate some useful intelligence, which I believe could be useful to you. I would like to firstly address the history of the various alliances that exist in Europe.

Triple Entente:

French and Russian diplomatic relations gradually developed through the late 1890s, and the Franco-Russian alliance of 1894 strengthened ties between the two countries. Anglo-French rivalry ended and cordial terms were established between Britain and France in 1904, when the two countries signed the Entente Cordiale.

Britain and Russia signed the Anglo-Russian Entente on August 31, 1907, at Saint Petersburg, Russia, ending traditional territorial conflict and defining the boundaries of Afghanistan, Tibet, and Persia. The alliance between France, Britain, and Russia that crystallized out of these three pacts is referred to as the Triple Alliance. It forms the backbone of the Allied Powers.

Triple Alliance:

The Dual Alliance as you would be aware was the treaty signed by Austria-Hungary on October 7, 1879. The alliance promised mutual support in case of a Russian attack. Italy, having lost the rivalry with France with regard to establishing the colony in Tunis, joined Germany and Austria-Hungary to form the Triple Alliance in 1882. Italy viewed the alliance as a guarantee against the invasion of Austria–Hungary, a rival nation. Italy also signed a guarantee of neutrality with Britain and later signed a similar guarantee pact with France.

In 1902 Britain made a naval treaty with Japan.

All the countries in the two alliances are building their armed forces at an alarming rate.

| | | |
|---|---|---|
| Germany | 2,200,000 soldiers | 97 Warships |
| Austria-Hungry | 810,000 soldiers | 28 Warships |
| Italy | 750,000 soldiers | 36 Warships |
| France | 1,125,000 soldiers | 62 Warships |
| Russia | 1,200,000 soldiers | 30 Warships |
| Britain | 711,000 soldiers | 185 Warships |

Some military analysts believe in a time of war these countries with the help of reservists could dramatically lift their numbers. An estimate is:

| | |
|---|---|
| Germany: | 8.5 million men |
| Austria-Hungary: | 3 million |
| Great Britain | 1.5 million |
| Russia: | 4.4 million |
| France: | 3.5 million |

There is no possible reason for such a build up other than to wage war. I firmly believe the Triple Alliance is on a war footing looking for an excuse to invade France.

Yours truly,

Captain Joseph Doherty

# 5.  The Garden Party

At last the day had arrived when the Dohertys were to attend the Garden Tea Party at Buckingham Palace. Joe had been at work at the Embassy for most of the day and arrived home at three in the afternoon to change into his dress uniform and escort Lucy to Buckingham Palace.

Lucy had been getting ready since ten that morning. She had planned her outfit down to what lingerie she would wear. The Embassy's brand new 1911 Cadillac was due to collect them at 3.30 pm and drop them off at the entrance.

At 3.30 p.m. sharp the car arrived and at 3.50 they were walking through Grosvenor Gardens Gate.

There were people everywhere walking in the gardens or talking in groups, but Lucy felt a little disappointed to see all these people attending - she felt her chances of actually meeting the Royals had diminished.

Joe and Lucy made their way to a white marquee to get a cup of tea and a dainty sandwich. They spoke to a few other visitors, mainly about the weather being so good for the occasion.

Suddenly the chitchat ceased as the King and Queen entered the gardens. It seemed a very informal walk through the gardens, chatting to their guests, with the odd smile or even laughter.

Joe and Lucy could not believe their eyes. The royal couple were heading their way and it seemed like the King was making a beeline for Joe. Sure enough both the King and Queen of England were standing directly in front of them.

'I see you are an American Naval Officer?'

'That's correct, your Majesty.'

'So, what brings you to our fair shores?'

'I am the Naval Attaché, Sir.'

'Are you now? So you would be very interested in our new Dreadnoughts, would you not?'

'They are a fine Battleship, Sir.'

'Yes, so I believe. What's your name, Captain?'

'Captain Joseph Doherty, Sir.'

'Irish stock no doubt. Captain, I would be keen to be briefed by you and get your opinion on where you see the naval build-up heading. Would you be available to come back next week?'

'Your Majesty, I would be honoured. I would need to get clearance from Naval HQ in Washington, but I am sure they would approve.'

'I'll get somebody in touch with you.'

'Good day to you Captain.'

For the entire time that King George was talking to Joe, the Queen was chatting to Lucy about America and how she enjoyed living in London. Lucy was over the moon and Joe didn't know what to think.

Lucy could not wait for the Friday Gin Rummy game so she could boast to her girl friends about her conversation with the Queen. Joe on the other hand did not mention his conservation with the King to anybody other than his commander in Washington.

He got approval with some provisos to meet with King George and discuss his views in relation to the naval build-up.

A message was delivered to the Embassy on the Monday following the garden party. It was from the King's secretary requesting he come to the palace the following Monday. He didn't disclose this to Lucy, as she would have trouble not divulging it to her friends. He would tell her after the meeting.

Joe arranged for an Embassy car to take him to the palace where he was met by Lieutenant-Colonel Arthur John Bigge, 1st Baron Stamfordham; the King's private secretary.

He was led down a magnificent hall to enter the King's private office. This was not just an office; it was quite large and had bookcases enclosing three sides. It overlooked some magnificent gardens. Various priceless paintings adorned the walls and the desk was something to behold - an eighteenth-century Chippendale originally made for King George III.

Captain Doherty was invited to sit on the leather lounge and wait for the King to appear. He didn't have to wait too long before George entered his office and shook the hand of the young American officer.

> 'Captain Doherty, the reason I asked you here was to discuss the alarming build-up of armed forces in Germany and her ally Austria-Hungary. I am also concerned about the Turks. I am sure your government is also alarmed, although perhaps not as concerned as we British.'

> 'What is it, your Majesty, that you wish from me?'

> 'Well, you are the Naval Attaché. You must be keeping a close eye on things, certainly from a naval point of view.'

> 'Yes Sir, my role is to ensure the United States interests are protected in this region. I therefore am required to report back to Washington any significant changes in fleet sizes and improvements in warship design.'

> 'Ah, so what have you reported back in relation to our new Dreadnoughts?'

> 'I reported back that these were the most modern powerful warships currently afloat.'

> 'Yes, they are a formidable war machine, aren't they?'

> 'They certainly are. That's why the Germans are rushing to build enough Dreadnoughts to bolster their own fleet.'

> 'Are they? I didn't know that. Captain, you have just made our meeting worthwhile. Are there any other nations building new battleships at a great rate?'

H.M. King George V's visit to the National Shell-Filling Factory (Chilwell Depot), 15 December 1916

'Certainly: Austria-Hungary, France and Italy. These nations don't yet have the numbers and will probably never get to Germany's fleet size.'

'What about Great Britain?'

'Great Britain has the largest fleet afloat and shall remain the largest for the foreseeable future. Britannia Rules the Waves.'

'Yes, of course. Thank you Captain. I have enjoyed our meeting. Most informative. Lieutenant-Colonel Bigge will show you out.'

Joe left the palace with a sense of bewilderment. Why hadn't his own Prime Minister briefed the King on the arms race in Europe? The King's level of knowledge could have been gained by any of his subjects reading *The Times*.

He decided not to tell Lucy about his private meeting with King George; he knew she would not be able to keep it confidential. He loved his wife madly, but knew her weakness was gossip. By the end of the week the whole of London and Washington would know.

King George V made it known to the Prime Minister that he was to be briefed on the build-up to World War I and right through the war.

**Under Ground Weapons Storage**

# 6.  Holiday

Joe was due for ten days leave, he and Lucy discussed the options – they could travel to Paris or they could take a train journey through England up to Scotland. They decided on England. After all, they had been living in the country for twelve months; they should see some of it.

They announced their plans to Jack and Julie who became quite excited about the prospect of travelling the country by train.

At last, after four weeks of anticipation the day came to travel to the train station to board *The Flying Scotsman*. Lucy had booked two co-joined sleepers.

Joe read to the family some of the history of Peterborough as the train steamed through it.

Peterborough began as a Saxon settlement. The Danes invaded it in 870 AD and then abandoned the settlement. In about 1000 AD a wall was built around the settlement to protect it from marauding Vikings. It was called St Peters Burgh. (Burgh was the Saxon word for a fortified settlement).

In 1070 AD an army of Danes (Vikings) and some Saxons attempted to overthrow William the Conqueror. They sacked the abbey at Peterborough and burned the town. However Peterborough soon recovered from the disaster and was rebuilt.

During the Middle Ages Peterborough was a small and relatively unimportant town controlled by the Abbot. The main industry was weaving wool.

When Henry VIII closed all the monasteries and abbeys in England, Peterborough Abbey was not excluded and it closed in 1539. However in 1541 the abbey church was reopened and made a cathedral. Also in 1541 Kings School was founded.

By the late 17$^{th}$ century the population had grown to around two thousand. The main industry in Peterborough was still wool manufacturing. But there was also some malting and from the 17$^{th}$ century clay pipes were made in Peterborough.

Like all towns in those days, Peterborough suffered outbreaks of plague. It struck in 1574, 1607, 1625 and 1665–67. Each time a significant part of the population died but Peterborough always recovered.

Mary Queen of Scots was buried in Peterborough Cathedral after her execution in 1587.

In 1643 during the civil war parliamentarian soldiers desecrated Peterborough Cathedral. They disapproved of images in churches and so they destroyed paintings and stone carvings. However the Old Guildhall was rebuilt in 1671.'


Joe finally realised his wife and children had fallen asleep. 'Not that interested in history,' he thought. 'Oh well, I think it's interesting.' He read the remainder of the chapters to himself.


The next historical city was York – surely they will be interested in the history of York. Our biggest city is named after it. We have a couple of hours before we arrive there and they'll be ready for another history lesson by then. As the locomotive was approaching York Joe pulled out his history of Britain book and started to recite. Lucy and the kids feigned interest.

York has changed hands several times in its history. It was founded by the pre-Roman Britons originally named Eborakon meaning 'place of the yew trees'. The Romans changed it to Eboracum in 71 AD and made it their capital. York became so important in Roman Britain that a palace was built in the city and the emperor Septimus Severus stayed there from 209-211. The most enduring legacy of the Romans is the city walls, around which you can still walk today.

The Romans left around 410 AD when the Anglo-Saxons who named the city Eoferwic replaced them. Little remains of the Saxons as their wooden buildings have not survived. Edwin, King of Northumbria constructed a church, especially to be baptised, and this is considered the first York Minster.

Roman City Walls

The Danish Vikings led by Ivar the Boneless, invaded York around the mid 9th century AD. The Vikings changed the name to Jorvik and left a legacy of street names behind. Gata in Danish means 'street', leading to current street names such as Micklegate and Castlegate. In the 11th Century, a succession of rebellions and invasions from Norway led England into the hands of the Normans.

William the Conqueror became King of England and medieval York became the base of his operations in the North. He built two castles, one on each side of the River Ouse. All that remains of these is the Northern Clifford's Tower. There were several uprisings against the Normans but these were suppressed with unprecedented savagery. Most tellingly, the population of Yorkshire fell from 8,000 to 2,000. The Normans also brought York into economic importance. The Minster was rebuilt in the Gothic style over the years 1220–1482, and the Archbishop of York was only second to the Archbishop of Canterbury in terms of religious influence.

At the end of this period, during the War of the Roses, York was a centre of power for the Lancastrian cause. Edward IV never forgave the city for being sympathetic to his enemy and ruled with an iron fist. The top of Micklegate Bar was decorated with the heads of the leaders. York's economic influence also began to ebb away at this time.

York also suffered under Henry VIII's reformation. In April 1644, York was besieged by parliamentary forces under the command of Sir Thomas Fairfax. King Charles' cousin Prince Rupert rushed to York's aid. However, York surrendered to the Parliamentary army. Many important buildings were destroyed but Fairfax convinced them to spare the Minster.

Joe decided that he would forgo the history lessons and let the family watch the scenery go by until they reached Edinburgh.

At last the locomotive steamed into Waverley station in Edinburgh where Lucy had arranged accommodation at what was reputed to be the finest hotel in the city: The North British Hotel. They settled into their suite and took a stroll along the famous Princes Street with its exclusive shops and lovely pubs and restaurants.

The Embassy had arranged a car to be available to them during their stay and good use was made of it. They toured all around Scotland taking in the lochs and mountains in the highlands. Joe even played a game of golf at the famous St Andrew's Course.

Finally their holiday was nearly at an end. They caught the train back to London and the next day Joe was at work and the children were at school. Lucy was once more having tea parties and playing cards with her friends.

# 7. Submarine

Joe was concerned that Britain seemed to be spending the entire naval defence budget on building bigger and faster battleships such as the Dreadnoughts whereas it seemed the Germans were slowing down on constructing battleships and concentrating on building submarines, or U-boats as the British called them. U-Boot was a shortening of *Unterseeboot*, which translates to 'undersea boat.'

Churchill quoted:

> 'The Admiralty had demanded six ships; the economists offered four; and we finally compromised on eight.'

Germany had completed and launched twenty U-Boats by the beginning of 1912. Surprisingly, Britain had over fifty but not of the sophistication of the German U-Boats.

Joe kept his commander in Washington up-to-date with what was happening in Europe; they both had concerns at the pace of the naval arms race. America was also building up its fleet in response. Under the President Theodore Roosevelt the US Navy grew from sixth largest in the world to second. Only Great Britain had a larger fleet.

Joe was convinced the Germans had it right in regards to the role of the submarine in modern naval warfare. Not only were the U-Boats the most sophisticated submarine afloat, they were the most deadly.

He believed the Germans would, if in a state of war, not only target Navy ships but also the civilian fleet, disrupting supplies and demoralising the civilian population.

In the early part of the 20th century America led the world in submarine technology but they had not continued to develop their advantage. As a result the American submarine fleet had fallen behind Britain, Germany and Japan.

Joe had made recommendations to Washington relating to developing new vessels but he had been largely ignored.

**U-Boats in Their Pen**

Confidential Report to Rear Admiral Eugene Leutze


23rd October 1911


Dear Sir,

The naval rivalry has played a major role in deepening the antagonism between Britain and Germany. I believe an arms control agreement designed to diminish the competition in shipbuilding may ease tensions and promote cooperation. I have met with Winston Churchill, First Lord of the Admiralty; he is in agreement that arms control would benefit both Great Britain and Germany. The British Government wish to improve Anglo-German relations. It is my understanding from the brief I received from Mr Churchill; Germany's leaders are not blind to the potential strategic advantages that might accrue to them from arms control. At this stage Britain and Germany have failed to achieve a negotiated solution to their naval competition, it was not for want of trying. I am convinced that both countries will continue to pursue naval arms control and for all our sakes I hope they are successful.

Winston used the term "a naval holiday" in describing his ambitions.

Yours truly,

Captain J Doherty

# 8. Leprechauns

Joe went home to Lucy and the kids with a plan in mind; they were due to leave Britain in four weeks' time, sailing home on the newly launched *Titanic* on her maiden voyage.

He called the family together in the parlour and announced that they were all going to sail to Ireland and discover their heritage. They would board the *Titanic* at Queenstown rather than Southampton.

The family were all excited by the prospect.

'When do we leave?' asked Julie.

'I thought two weeks' touring so I guess that means we leave London in two weeks.'

'Oh my God, I have hardly started to pack,' Lucy cried with panic in her voice.

'Don't worry Darling. We'll make it.'

'I hope you're right.'

They all started to think about what needed to happen before the twenty-eighth of March when they were due to sail to Ireland.

The days went quickly. Lucy and the children were responsible for packing up the house while Joe was responsible for organising the logistics of the holiday and handing the reins over to his replacement, Frank Woods. Captain Woods was quite disturbed by the briefings Joe gave him but at least he was aware of the trouble brewing.

At last the day of departure arrived and they were due to board the steamship *Columbia*.

The journey only took a day and night and before they knew it they had stepped onto Irish soil. The Doherty family had a very strong and ancient history in Ireland. Joe read from the book he had purchased in London.

> The Doherty family (Irish: Clann Dhochartaigh) is an Irish clan based in County Donegal in the north of the island of Ireland.

> Like clans in other cultures, Irish clans such as the Dohertys are divided into many septs and regional families. In the modern day, there are 140 noted variations in spelling of the name Ó Dochartaigh, of which Doherty (with or without the 'Ó') is the most common anglicisation.

> The Doherty's are named after Dochartach, the 12th in linear descent from Conall Gulban (d. AD 455), the son of the famous Niall of the Nine Hostages (Niall Noigíallach) the 5th Century High King of Ireland, and namesake of the powerful Uí Néill dynasty. Through Niall, the Dohertys can trace their heritage back even further, making the clan one of Europe's longest descent lines. The origins of the family however, as with the Irish people and their ancestors, the Gaels, are obscured by Celtic mythology and folk tales.'

The American Embassy had once again arranged a motor vehicle, which was waiting for them near the dock. Their first night would be spent in Dublin at Ariel House, a beautiful Victorian hotel in the heart of the city.

The next day the family headed off to Killarney, south west of Dublin. Why Ireland is called the Emerald Isle became evident as they drove through the lush countryside. Passing the River Liffey they arrived at the imposing Rock of Cashel, which was apparently the seat of the Kings of Munster, according to Joe's travel book. The next stop was Blarney Castle where they all kissed the

Blarney Stone hoping to receive its magical powers of speech. The group stayed in Killarney that night at a beautiful country hotel, Woodlawn House.

After a scrumptious breakfast they headed off to Ennis, taking in the magnificent scenery of the Dingle Peninsula with its ancient castles and Celtic fortifications. Joe was a little concerned that Jack and Julie might find this holiday a tad boring but they were enjoying it so far. The mighty Shannon River had to be crossed before they arrived at their destination, Ennis. They stayed at a beautiful old hotel, The Old Ground.

Next morning Joe drove to the legendary Cliffs of Moher rising hundreds of feet above the Atlantic Ocean; the same ocean they would be sailing on back to America in a few days.

Julie had hoped she would see a leprechaun while in Ireland and where they were travelling to now, Burren, was the reputed home of these magical creatures.

Greagan's Castle was the hotel they stayed in and it was magnificent – an eighteenth century manor house surrounded by beautiful gardens.

Then they were off to Inis Mór the largest of the Aran Islands. When he arrived in Britain, Joe was impressed with the ubiquitous stonewalls – Inis Mór had over three thousand miles of superbly constructed stonewalls.

The kids were keen to hire a horse and cart to explore the island and that's what they did. This really was an experience they would all remember. The next destination was Galway and then on to Limerick and finally Queenstown, where they would board the *Titanic*, which was something the entire family was looking forward to. Their hotel, Hayfield Manor, was fantastic – an eighteenth century hotel with all the modern facilities including ensuite bathrooms.

**The *Titanic* Docking at Queenstown**

The next morning, Thursday 11th April, Joe, Lucy, Jack and Julie caught a taxi to the Queenstown dock. They could see the ship before they reached its berth: it was huge.

'No wonder they named her the *Titanic,*' exclaimed Jack.

Joe reported into the ticket office with his four first-class tickets. A porter arranged to help with the family's luggage, which was quite considerable, mainly due to Lucy's spending while in London. The family had two cabins next to each other and they soon settled in and went off to explore the ship. Jack and Lucy could not believe the size or the luxury – it really was a five-star hotel afloat.

The next three days were spent enjoying the first-class facilities. Jack and Julie had fun in the swimming pool while Joe availed himself of the excellent gymnasium. He also found a partner to challenge him in a game of squash. After all that physical activity an hour in the Turkish bath soothed sore muscles. Lucy just enjoyed hearing the background music of the ship's orchestra and playing cards with some of the other passengers.

# 15<sup>th</sup> April, 1912

Joe had just completed a session in the gym and entered the cabin hoping for a quiet relaxing time before they went up for dinner. He entered the cabin only to find Lucy dressed in one of her finest outfits and busily applying makeup.

**First Class Gymnasium**

'So my love, what's going on? Did we get an invitation to a wedding or something?'

'Don't be silly Darling. No, we have been invited to dine with the Captain at his table. He requested you wear your dress uniform. You did pack it, didn't you?'

'Yes, I packed it. Can't we decline? Say I'm sick or something?'

'No we can't! Now get dressed.'

Jack and Julie were also invited to the table; they were much more enthusiastic than their father.

The family entered the dining room and the head waiter escorted them to the

# First-Class Menu

**FIRST COURSE — HORS D'OEUVRE**
Canapés à l'Amiral
Oysters à la Russe
White Bordeaux, White Burgundy or
Chablis (especially with oysters)

**SECOND COURSE — SOUPS**
Consommé Olga
Cream of Barley Soup
Madeira or Sherry

**THIRD COURSE — FISH**
Poached Salmon with Mousseline Sauce
Dry Rhine or Moselle

**FOURTH COURSE — ENTRÉES**
Filets Mignons Lili
Chicken Lyonnaise
Vegetable Marrow Farci
Red Bordeaux

**FIFTH COURSE — REMOVES**
Lamb with Mint Sauce
Calvados-Glazed Roast Duckling
with Applesauce
Roast Sirloin of Beef Forestière
Château Potatoes
Minted Green Pea Timbales
Creamed Carrots
Boiled Rice
Parmentier and Boiled New Potatoes
Red Burgundy or Beaujolais

**SIXTH COURSE — PUNCH OR SORBET**
Punch Romaine

**SEVENTH COURSE — ROAST**
Roasted Squab on Wilted Cress
Red Burgundy

**EIGHTH COURSE — SALAD**
Asparagus Salad with Champagne-
Saffron Vinaigrette

**NINTH COURSE — COLD DISH**
Pâté de Foie Gras
Celery
Sauterne or Sweet Rhine Wine

**TENTH COURSE — SWEETS**
Waldorf Pudding
Peaches in Chartreuse Jelly
Chocolate Painted Eclairs
with French Vanilla Cream
French Vanilla Ice Cream
Sweet Dessert Wines (Muscatel, Tokay, Sauterne)

**ELEVENTH COURSE — DESSERT**
Assorted fresh fruits and cheeses
Sweet Dessert Wines, Champagne, or Sparkling Wine

**AFTER DINNER**
Coffee, cigars
Port or Cordials

Captain's Table where Captain Smith and a few of his officers were already seated. Four more guests were due to join them including Benjamin Guggenheim who was a wealthy industrialist and heir to the Guggenheim mining fortune and J. Bruce Ismay, the chairman and managing director of the

White Star Line who was the person who sketched the first plans for the *Titanic* on a dinner napkin in 1907.

Colonel John Jacob Astor IV and his pregnant wife Madeleine Astor were also guests and were the last to be seated. Astor was a much-respected real estate multi-millionaire.

There was a sense of excitement at the table everybody agreed the maiden voyage of the *Titanic* had been a magnificent success and the ship had lived up to all the publicity. There was also the excitement of berthing in New York. Joe asked the Captain what was their current speed?

> 'We were doing twenty three knots but have slowed down to twenty two.'

> 'That's a good speed Sir, particularly with the number of passengers on board. The bridge must be something else Captain.'

> 'Captain Doherty, would you care to join me on the bridge? The equipment we have installed is state-of-the-art. I think you will enjoy the experience.'

> 'Certainly Captain Smith, I would be honoured Sir.'

# 9. Life Without Joe

The three Doherty survivors were rescued by one of *Carpathia*'s lifeboats and the crew rowed them to the side of the ship where they were winched up to one of the decks. There were many crew and passengers there to assist them once on board. They were given blankets and taken to a row of deck chairs. This is where they would sleep on the voyage to New York.

*Carpathia* took three days to reach New York after leaving the scene of the disaster. Pack ice, fog, thunderstorms and rough seas hampered her journey. The ship's Captain, Arthur Rostron, authorised the radio room to pass news on to the outside world via wireless regarding what had happened. The initial reports were confused, leading the American press to report erroneously on 15th April 'that the SS *Virginian* was towing *Titanic* to port'. Later that day, confirmation came through that *Titanic* had been lost and that most of her passengers and crew had died. The news attracted crowds of people to the White Star Line's offices in London, New York, Southampton and Belfast. The news hit hardest in Southampton, where people suffered the greatest losses from the sinking. Four out of five crewmembers came from this town. *Carpathia* docked at 9.30 pm on 18th April at New York's Pier 54 and was greeted by some forty thousand people waiting at the quayside in heavy rain. The Women's Relief Committee, the Travellers' Aid Society of New York, and the Council of Jewish Women, plus various other organisations provided immediate relief in the form of clothing and transportation to shelters. Many of *Titanic*'s surviving passengers did not linger in New York but headed onwards immediately to relatives' homes. Some of the wealthier survivors chartered private trains to take them home, and the Pennsylvania Railroad laid on a special train free of charge to take survivors to Philadelphia. *Titanic*'s two hundred and four surviving crewmembers were taken to the Red Star Line's steamer SS *Lapland*, where they were accommodated in passenger cabins.

Lucy and the children were fortunate to have her mother and father greet them as they lived close by in New Jersey. For the first time in what seemed an eternity they all slept in clean sheets and warm dry blankets. The most memorable moment was having a hot bath. Their grief and sorrow coming from losing their father and husband would take a long time to subside.

Lucy and the children stayed in New Jersey for a few weeks and although grateful for the kindness and hospitality they all felt it was time to move back to Chesapeake and try and get on with their lives.

John and Jennifer Broderick drove the family to the train station kissed their daughter and grandchildren goodbye, promising to visit them later in the year.

When Lucy and the children first unlocked and entered the family home they all began to cry. How could they live in this house without Joe? He was the patriarch, the advisor, the joker and the one that encouraged his children to always strive to do their best.

Lucy knew it was going to be very difficult but they had no other choice than to move on and live their lives as best they could.

Jack and Julie returned to school and soon fitted into the routine. Jack ambitiously tried to teach his class how to play cricket, however he failed to convince them that this strange game should ever replace baseball.

The years rolled by and life went on without Joe. Lucy received great support from Gene Leutze, Joe's commanding officer. Support became love and three years after Joe was lost the couple got married. It was a good match. Lucy enjoyed the life of an Admiral's wife in Washington, being invited to the White House and meeting the President and First Lady. Gene loved having Lucy by his side on these occasions – she was the ultimate socialite.

Jack had thought long and hard about joining the Navy but had trouble coming to grips with the way his father died. He had developed a real fear of drowning at sea – not what he needed to become a career naval officer. Ultimately he decided a career in the armed services would be his chosen path and he enrolled at West Point.

**Graduate Class of 1917**

Julie had decided to pursue a career in medicine. She enrolled at Temple University School of Medicine in Pennsylvania in 1914, graduating in 1918.

Jack revelled in the academy lifestyle and excelled in all his classes apart from mathematics. Lucy and Gene employed a maths tutor and with a lot of tuition and hard work he passed his final maths exam. His real interest lay in battle tactics and foreign languages and he became fluent in French and German.

The two siblings had no real idea what awaited them in the very near future. Events in Europe were about to change their plans and aspirations forever.

# 10. Black Hand Red Blood

*Daddy, how did the First World War Start?*

## Events Leading Up to the Assassination of Prince Franz Ferdinand and Sophie

Bosnia and Herzegovina were provinces south of Austria which had until 1878, been governed by the Turks. The Treaty of Berlin settled the disposition of lands lost by the Turks following their disastrous war with Russia. Austria was granted the power to administer the two provinces indefinitely.

Primarily four groups populated Bosnia: Croats predominantly Roman Catholic; ethnic Serbs; Serb-Orthodox and Muslims.

There was a strong desire by the Bosnian Serbs to amalgamate with Serbia.

## The Annexation

On 6<sup>th</sup> October 1908, Austria annexed Bosnia and Herzegovina directly into the Austro-Hungarian Empire. The reasons were twofold.

Annexation would remove any hope the Turks might have for reclaiming the provinces. Full inclusion into the empire would give Bosnians full rights and privileges.

The annexation caused concern to a number of Europe's powers. The move was regarded by some as illegal. Russia was particularly concerned by the move despite previously giving approval to the annexation.

After tough negotiations Austria paid Turkey a cash settlement. This seemed to placate most of Europe.

The Serbs, however, were not happy. They coveted the provinces to expand the Serb empire.

## The Black Hand

The Black Hand was established to spread anti-Austrian propaganda within Serbia as well as sabotage, espionage and political murders abroad. This terrorist group included many government officials, professionals and army officers.

The Black Hand became aware that the heir-apparent to the Austrian throne, Franz Ferdinand, was scheduled to visit Sarajevo in June of 1914 – it was decided to assassinate him. Three young Bosnians were recruited, trained and equipped: Gavrilo Princip, Nedjelko Cabrinovic and Trifko Grabez.

## The Serbian Government

Because the Black Hand had infiltrated both the government and the army, the plot became widely known. When the Serbian Prime Minister Pasic learned of the assassination plot, he faced a difficult decision. If he remained silent and the plot succeeded, the Black Hand's involvement would be revealed. If the clandestine connections between the Black Hand and the Serbian government came to light Serbia would be put in a very onerous position. There would be a very real chance that war between the two nations would erupt.

His problem was that if he warned the Austrians of the plot, his countrymen would see him as a traitor. He would also be admitting to his knowledge of Black Hand's operations.

A half-hearted attempt was made to intercept the assassins at the border. When that failed, Pasic decided diplomacy should be attempted.

The Serbian Ambassador to Vienna, Jovan Jovanovic, was given the task of warning the Austrians. He was aligned with Black Hand and was not well received by the Austrian Foreign Ministry. He did, however, have a good relationship with the Minister of Finance, Dr Leon von Bilinski.

On 5th June Jovanovic told Bilinski that it might not be a good idea if Franz Ferdinand went to Sarajevo.

> 'Some young Serb might put a live rather than a blank cartridge in his gun and fire it.'

Bilinski, unaccustomed to subtle diplomatic innuendo, completely missed the warning. 'Let us hope nothing does happen,' he responded good-humouredly.

Jovanovic knew that Bilinski did not understand, but made no further effort to convey the warning.

## Preparations

The three Black Hand assassins secretly made their way to Sarajevo a month before Franz Ferdinand was due to visit. A fourth man, Danilo Ilic, had joined the group and on his own initiative recruited three others. Vaso Cubrilovic and Cvijetko Popovic were seventeen-year-old high school students. Muhamed Mehmedbasic, a Bosnian Muslim, was added to give the group a bipartisan appearance. Officers from the Serbian army supplied four Serbian army pistols and six bombs.

## Prince Franz Ferdinand and Sophie's Royal Visit

Franz Ferdinand accepted the invitation of Bosnia's governor, General Oskar Potoirek, to inspect army manoeuvres outside Sarajevo. The Archduke's role as Inspector General of the Army made the visit logical. It had also been four years since a prominent Royal had made a goodwill visit to Bosnia.

The visit would also coincide with his fourteenth wedding anniversary. Security during the visit was not particularly tight. Franz Ferdinand disliked the presence of secret service men. Nor did he like the idea of a cordon of soldiers between the crowd and himself. The Bosnians welcomed Franz Ferdinand warmly. Sarajevo was not seen as hostile territory; the normal police guard was present, nothing more.

## 28th June 1914

At approximately 10:00 am the Austrian party left Philipovic army camp, where Franz Ferdinand had performed a brief review of the troops. The motorcade, consisting of six automobiles, headed for City Hall where a reception was to be hosted by Sarajevo's mayor. The chosen route was a wide avenue, Appel Quay, which followed the north bank of the River Miljacka.

In the first automobile rode the Mayor Fehim Effendi Curcic and the city's Commissioner of Police, Dr Gerde. The second automobile was a 1911 Gräf &

Stift Double Phaeton. It had its top folded down and was flying the Royal Hapsburg pennant. This was the vehicle Franz Ferdinand, Sophie and General Potoirek were travelling in. The car's owner, Count Harrach, rode on the car's running board acting as a bodyguard for the Royal couple.

**Minutes before the Assassination**

The third automobile in the procession carried the head of Franz Ferdinand's Military Chancellery; Sophie's lady-in-waiting; Potoirek's chief adjutant; Lieutenant Colonel Merizzi; the car's owner Count Harrach and his driver. The fourth and fifth automobiles carried other members of Franz Ferdinand's staff and assorted Bosnian officials. The sixth automobile was empty, a spare should one of the others break down.

The morning was sunny and warm and many of the houses and buildings lining the route were decorated with flags and flowers. Crowds lined the Appel Quay to cheer the imperial couple. Amid the festive crowd lurked seven young assassins. They took up their assigned positions, all but one along the riverside of the Appel Quay. First in line was Mehmedbasic, to the west of the Cumurja Bridge. Near him was Cabrinovic. The others were strung out as far back as the Kaiser Bridge.

## The Bomb

The motorcade approached and the crowds began to cheer. As Franz Ferdinand's car passed Mehmedbasic, he did nothing. The next assassin in line, Cabrinovic, had more resolve. He took the bomb from his coat pocket, struck the bomb's percussion cap against a lamppost, took aim and threw the bomb directly at Franz Ferdinand.

In the short time it took the bomb to sail through the air, many small but significant events took place. The car's owner, Count Harrach, hearing the bomb being struck against the lamppost thought they had suffered a flat tyre. The driver apparently saw the bomb flying. He reacted quickly, accelerating away from the scene. As a result of the driver's quick thinking the bomb would not land where intended. Franz Ferdinand raised his arm attempting to deflect the bomb away from Sophie.

The bomb glanced off Franz Ferdinand's arm, bouncing off the folded car top and into the street behind them. The resulting explosion injured a number of spectators. The third car was hit by shrapnel and stalled. Merizzi received head injuries. Others in the party received minor cuts. The first and second cars continued on for a hundred metres or so, then stopped while they assessed who was injured.

## The Aftermath

Cabrinovic attempted to commit suicide but the cyanide capsule was well and truly past its use-by date – he just vomited, then jumped into the river hoping to drown. This proved futile, as the river was only a few inches deep.

He was seized by the crowd and arrested by the police. The motorcade continued on to City Hall, passing the other assassins on route. Not one of them attempted to assassinate the Royal couple.

At City Hall, a furious Franz Ferdinand confronted the Mayor.

'Mr Mayor, one comes here for a visit and is received by bombs! It is outrageous!'

The Mayor was either completely unaware of what had happened, or naïve.

'Your Royal and Imperial Highness! Our hearts are full of happiness...'

By the end of the Mayor's speech, Franz Ferdinand had regained his composure and thanked his host for his cordial welcome.

*'There is no chance, no destiny, no fate that can circumvent or hinder or control the firm resolve of a determined soul.'*

Ella Wheeler Wilcox

Discussions were held as to whether to abandon Franz Ferdinand's schedule. The Archduke did not wish to cancel his visit to the museum and the lunch at the Governor's residence. One change he wished to make was to include a visit to Merizzi in the hospital: he was very concerned for Merizzi.

The motorcade set out once again along the Appel Quay, but neither the Mayor's driver nor Franz Ferdinand's driver had been informed of the change in schedule.

The young Black Hand assassins had counted on succeeding on the first attempt. With no assurance that Franz Ferdinand would follow his original itinerary, the remaining assassins took up various other positions along the Appel Quay. Gavrilo Princip crossed the Appel Quay and strolled down Franz Josef Street. He stepped into Moritz Schiller's food store to get a sandwich. As he emerged, he met a friend and engaged in light conversation.

# Fate Plays its Part

The Mayor's car, followed by Franz Ferdinand's turned off the Appel Quay and onto Franz Josef Street, as originally planned, to travel to the museum. General Potoirek leaned forward.

'What is this? This is the wrong way! We're supposed to take the Appel Quay!'

The driver applied the brakes and backed up. Franz Ferdinand's car stopped directly in front of Schiller's store, five feet away from Princip, the assassin.

## An Opportunity Too Good to be True

Princip was quick to recognise what had happened. He pulled the pistol from his pocket, took a step towards the car and fired twice. General Potoirek happened to look directly at Princip as he fired.

Both Franz Ferdinand and Sophie were still sitting upright. Potoirek, thinking the shots had missed, ordered the driver to drive directly to the Governor's residence at speed.

Princip then turned the gun on himself, but was mobbed by the crowd. Police were able to arrest him. Princip also attempted suicide by swallowing cyanide. He too was violently ill, but did not die.

## Mortal Wounds

As the car sped across the Lateiner Bridge, a stream of blood shot from Franz Ferdinand's mouth. He had been shot in the neck. Sophie, seeing this, exclaimed: 'For Heaven's sake! What happened to you?'

She sank down in her seat. Potoirek and Harrach thought she had fainted and were trying to help her up. Franz Ferdinand, knowing his wife better, suspected the truth. Sophie had been shot in the abdomen and was bleeding internally.

> 'Sopherl! Sopherl!' he pleaded. *'Sterbe nicht! Bleibe am Leben für unsere Kinder!'* ('Sophie dear! Sophie dear! Don't die! Stay alive for our children!')

The cars rushed to the Governor's residence. Sophie died before they arrived. Franz Ferdinand died shortly afterward.

## The Horrific Result

On 23rd July the Austro-Hungarian Ambassador to Serbia delivered an ultimatum:

'The Serbian government must take steps to wipe out terrorist organisations within its borders, suppress anti-Austrian propaganda and accept an independent investigation by the Austro-Hungarian government into Franz Ferdinand's assassination, or face military action.'

Serbia appealed to Russia for help; the Czar's government began moving towards mobilisation of its army, believing that Germany was using the crisis as an excuse to launch a war in the Balkans. Austria-Hungary declared war on Serbia on 28th July. On 1st August, after hearing news of Russia's general mobilisation, Germany declared war on Russia. The German Army then launched its attack on Russia's ally France through Belgium, violating Belgian neutrality and bringing Great Britain into the war.

**EXTRA!**    **THE** 🦅 **ONION**    **EXTRA!**

Wednesday, August 5, 1914    The Best Source of News    in Our Great Republic    Price Five Cents

# WAR DECLARED BY ALL

## AUSTRIA DECLARES WAR ON SERBIA DECLARES WAR ON GERMANY DECLARES WAR ON FRANCE DECLARES WAR ON TURKEY DECLARES WAR ON RUSSIA DECLARES WAR ON BULGARIA DECLARES WAR ON BRITAIN

### OTTOMAN EMPIRE ALMOST DECLARES WAR ON ITSELF

### NATIONS STRUGGLE TO REMEMBER ALLIES

ASSASSINATION OF ARCHDUKE SPARKS FEAR AT ARCHDUKE CONVENTION

### AREA DRUNKARD DECLARES WAR ON IRELAND

#### ALE-HOUSE FIEND FALLS IN AS ALLIES

# 11. You Never Know What You're Going to Get

The war in Europe had been going for over two years when Jack graduated as Second Lieutenant.

The United States President, Woodrow Wilson, was very reluctant to enter World War I. He declared US neutrality and insisted that both sides respect America's rights as a neutral country.

Americans were deeply divided about the war in Europe, and how involvement could disrupt progressive reforms. 'Top of the Pops' at the time was *I Didn't Raise My Boy to be a Soldier*.

In 1916 Wilson narrowly won re-election with a slogan 'He kept us out of the war'.

Although claiming neutrality, it became clear that the US began to lean towards Britain and France.

Wilson knew that wartime trade with the belligerents was important to the American economy; trade boomed with the Allies.

The cash reserves of the Allies and the Germans were being eaten up by the war effort. They asked the USA for a line of credit and so in October 1915, President Wilson approved loans to both sides, although the Allies were the biggest benefactors. Loans to the Allies totalled $2.25 billion by 1917. On the other hand, Germany had outstanding loans of $27 million.

Germany announced a resumption of unrestricted submarine warfare in January 1917, which was an extremely provocative move, particularly after Germany sank the *Lusitania* in 1915, killing almost two thousand people – many of them were Americans.

Germany was bullish about winning the war within five months and therefore even if America entered the conflict it could not mobilise quickly enough to change the course of the war; or so Germany thought.

What really pushed Wilson to the limit of his patience was the 'Zimmerman Telegram', a telegram which said that if Mexico went to war with the United States, Germany promised to help Mexico recover the territory it had lost during the 1840s, including Texas, New Mexico, California and Arizona.

The telegram and the fact that Germany attacked three US ships during March led Wilson to ask Congress for a 'declaration of war'.

In 1917, a senior German official scoffed at American might: 'America from a military point-of-view means nothing, and again nothing, and for a third time nothing.' The US Army at the time had only 107,641men.

Within a year, however, the United States raised a five million-man army. By the war's end, the American armed forces were a decisive factor in blunting a German offensive and ending the bloody stalemate.

To raise troops, President Wilson insisted on a military draft. More than twenty-three million men registered during World War I; and two million, eight hundred thousand draftees served in the armed forces. To select officers, the army launched an ambitious program of psychological testing.

Jack certainly didn't sit for any psychological testing; he was an officer with the US Marines.

He boarded the troop ship *Carpathia* at Hoboken on 13th June 1917. He couldn't believe he was back on the ship that saved his sister, mother and himself after the *Titanic* sank. This had to be good omen. He disembarked at St Nazaire on 26th June. With him were his best buddy John Younger and fourteen thousand American troops all arriving on various ships around about the same time. These troops would come to be known as 'Doughboys'.

(Doughboy is an informal term for a member of the United States Army or Marine Corps, especially members of the American Expeditionary Forces in World War I. They were widely memorialised through the mass production of a sculpture, the Spirit of the American Doughboy. The term dates back to the Mexican–American War of 1846–48.)

The whole operation had been top secret, as the American High Command didn't want to alert German U-Boats. Nevertheless when they landed, a large and enthusiastic French crowd had gathered to welcome them.

General Pershing had been appointed as the Chief Commander of the American Expeditionary Force. He was well aware that his troops were very green and required more training. He established training camps and organised the supply networks very soon after he arrived in France. He also established the communication networks.

# 21$^{st}$ October 1917

# Luneville France

The first American soldiers entered combat when they were assigned to enter Allied trenches in the Luneville sector near Nancy. Each American unit was attached to a corresponding French unit. Two days later, Lieutenant Jack Doherty was the first American to fire a shot in anger when he discharged a French 75mm gun into a German trench five hundred metres away.

On 2$^{nd}$ November Corporal Thomas Enright and Private Merle Hay of the 16$^{th}$ Infantry became the first American soldiers to die when Germans raided their trenches near Bathelemont.

'Johnnie, how are you going buddy? Handling it okay?'

'Yeah, I'm fine. Not much happening, is there? I thought we would be in full on combat most of the time, not sitting around this grungy trench with Frenchies who can't talk to you. Not in English anyway.'

'Yeah, I know what you mean. It's hard keeping the men alert while we're waiting for something to happen.'

'Holy shit, the bastards are firing shells at us. Keep your head down and make sure your men do the same.'

**US Soldiers Waiting in the Trench**

The German artillery was starting to find its targets. Shells were exploding in the trenches and American soldiers were being blown to hell.

The French Captain assigned to their unit spoke some English. He explained to Jack and John that as soon as the barrage ceased there would be an infantry attack; they and their men needed to be prepared.

Sure enough, the shells stopped and through their periscopes they could see Krauts running towards the Allied positions, firing as they went.

Jack ordered his machine gunners to fire when they had the bastards in their sights. The Lewis machine guns opened fire almost in unison along the line of trenches. Jack could see the Germans dropping like flies but more of the bastards came up from the rear to replace the fallen. This was not going to be easy. The Boche was finding it difficult to make real headway, as no man's land was a pock-marked muddy moonscape and the intensity of the US and French fire meant the Germans became bogged down.

Eventually, the orders came through to the German officers to pull their men back to their own lines.

Jack observed this happening through his periscope and notified his commanding officer, Captain Phillip Cosser. Captain Cosser notified Infantry Command to shell the retreating Krauts and gave them the coordinates. They were to commence the barrage immediately and cease firing twenty minutes later. His plan was to then go over the top and attack the Germans while they were still in no mans land.

The allied inventory began to create havoc, with Germans being slaughtered across the muddy bog. The smell of fresh blood and torn flesh permeated across to the American trenches causing some of these fresh inexperienced troops to be physically ill.

Twenty minutes had passed and the big guns ceased firing their deadly shells. The order was given, the whistles blew and the troops climbed the ladders and started across no man's land in pursuit of the enemy. The Krauts had bunkered down in shell craters and old foxholes trying to avoid the American artillery. It was here they created a new line to foil the American-French advance.

The opposing armies were now in open warfare, exposed without any real shelter or protection.

Jack and John and some of the men they led were in a large shell crater, with two Lewis machineguns, which were firing relentlessly at the German positions.

The Germans were proving to be extremely difficult to eliminate and Captain Cosser sent a runner back to the allied trench with a message requesting the artillery give the bastards another pounding.

Suddenly shells began dropping and exploding all around them.

'Fucking Germans! They'll not only kill us – they'll kill their own!' screamed Jack.

John looked around. 'Jack, they're not German shells. They're coming from our boys. The stupid bastards have got the coordinates wrong!'

The artillery almost destroyed the allied troops and allowed the Germans to return to their trenches to fight another day.

Incredibly Jack and Johnno survived the so-called 'friendly fire' and slowly returned to their own trench. A count was taken: Captain Cosser estimated seventy per cent of their troops had been killed. He figured most of these deaths occurred due to their own artillery.

**The Aftermath of Battle**

*'It takes five thousand deaths to train artillery to be accurate.'*

Captain Phillip Cosser

# 12. Uncle Sam's Victory

In March 1918, the Germans launched a massive offensive on the Western Front in France's Somme River valley. With German troops barely fifty miles from Paris, Marshal Ferdinand Foch, the leader of the French army, assumed command of the allied forces. Foch's troops, aided by eighty-five thousand American soldiers, launched a furious counter-offensive. By the end of October, the counterattack pushed the German army back to the Belgian border.

American entry into the war quickly overcame the German military's numerical advantage. In June 1918, some two hundred and seventy nine thousand American soldiers crossed the Atlantic; in July over three hundred thousand; in August, two hundred and eighty six thousand more. All told, one and a half million American troops arrived in Europe during the last six months of the war. By the end of the conflict, the Allies could field six hundred thousand more men than the Germans at any one time.

The next action for Jack and Johnno would come at Belleau Wood.

The American actions took place firstly at Chateau-Thierry from $3^{rd}$ to the $4^{th}$ June and then at Belleau Wood itself from $6^{th}$ to the $26^{th}$ June. The Battle of Belleau Wood saw the Wood finally re-captured by US forces.

Chateau-Thierry formed the tip of the German advance towards Paris, some fifty miles southwest. Defended by US Second and Third Divisions dispatched at the behest of the French by AEF Commander-in-Chief, Jack Pershing, the Americans launched a counter-attack on $3^{rd}$ and $4^{th}$ June with the assistance of the French Tenth Colonial Division. In a spirited action together they succeeded in pushing the Germans back across the Marne to Jaulgonne.

Rejuvenated by success first at Cantigny at the end of May and now at Chateau-Thierry, General Bundy's Second Division forces followed up Chateau-Thierry two days later with the difficult exercise of capturing Belleau Wood.

Second Division's Marine Corps, under James Harbord, was tasked with the taking of the Wood. This perilous venture involved a murderous trek across an open wheat field, strafed from end to end by German machine gun fire, a fact that continues to generate controversy today among some historians.

As a consequence of the open nature of the advance on the Wood, casualties on the first day, the 6th June, were the highest in Marine Corps history (a dubious record which remained until the capture of Japanese-held Tarawa in November 1943).

**Marine Inspecting German Gun Placement**

Fiercely defended by the Germans, the Wood was first taken by the Marines (and Third Infantry Brigade), then ceded back to the Germans – and again taken by the US forces a total of six times before the Germans were finally expelled. Also captured were the nearby villages of Vaux and Bouresche.

The battle ran from the 1st to the 26th June and by its end, US forces suffered 9,777 casualties, of which 1,811 were fatal. The number of German casualties is not known, although some 1,600 troops were taken prisoner. More critically, the combined Chateau-Thierry/Belleau Wood action brought to an end the last major German offensive of the war.

The French name for the wood, Bois Belleau, was subsequently officially renamed Bois de la Brigade de Marine, in honour of the Marine Corps' tenacity.'

**The Wood**

# 13. If You Go Down to the Woods Today

## You're in For a Big Surprise

6<sup>th</sup> June 1918

## Belleau Wood

Jack found himself alone, not in the true sense of the word, but alone without Johnnie. His best mate had been killed the day before. They were ordered to enter Belleau and eliminate or at least drive off the Germans who were holed up in just one corner of the Wood. Their unit; the 4<sup>th</sup> Marine Brigade were ordered to advance straight ahead into the Wood then come around and flank the German troops. The actual situation was that the Krauts had the whole Wood covered and had ample machine guns to kill every last marine, which was their intention.

They nearly did. The casualty rate was enormous. Jack was lucky to survive the fight; not so Johnnie.

Jack was waiting for the order to advance and looked around at his men – they all looked very pensive, if not shit-scared. The first assault by the 1<sup>st</sup> Battalion 5<sup>th</sup> Marine Regiment had begun their day early at 5 am. The word came back that they had been successful in capturing Hill 142. This was a strategic position as these boys could support the 4<sup>th</sup> Marine Brigade's assault on the Wood, the assault he and his boys were just about to undertake.

Jack, his men, and the rest of the 5<sup>th</sup> and 6<sup>th</sup> Marine Battalions had been waiting all day for the order to go. It was now 5 pm. Their objective was capturing the village of Bouresches. The order was given and they began crossing a very expansive wheat field.

The German machine guns hidden strategically in the wood had a clear view of the attacking Marines and French troops. They were mowed down like wheat, their red blood staining the fields of gold. By the end of the first attack the Allies had secured a small section of their overall objective.

Jack was approaching the first line of trees when he felt a sharp pain and a ripping sensation through his chest. He started to turn as if in slow motion; he wanted to go home now. The horrendous noise of battle became a distant hum. He fell to his knees, then lay down. He did not move again.

The French had been using dogs to support their war effort since 1914. They used them as messenger dogs, ambulance dogs, guard dogs – even cigarette dogs.

After the hell of the first day at Belleau Wood the French commander Jacques Pétain gave orders for the ambulance dogs to be dispatched to the battlefield and determine if there were any wounded that could be retrieved and saved by the stretcher bearers.

One such dog was named Michael. He was a Curly-Coated Retriever and had already been awarded medals for bravery. All armies awarded dogs medals for bravery.

Michael was sent out with eight other dogs to search. He discovered Jack stretched out amongst the sheafs of wheat. He sniffed Jack's entire body and decided he was alive and could be retrieved. Michael and the other dogs were trained to grab a piece of clothing from the wounded soldier, taking it back to their line. The stretcher-bearers would then follow the dog back to the wounded soldier. A medical officer would complete a quick assessment and decide if the wounded soldier was 'alive enough' to take back to the dressing station.

Michael grabbed a handkerchief from the top left pocket of Jack's uniform. This was no ordinary handkerchief; it had belonged to his father, Jack, who always carried it with him while on duty. Michael ran back to the French line, the handkerchief firmly in his grasp.

'Michael, lead!' the commander of the medical team said.

Following the black dog as closely as they could, they finally came across Jack. The doctor examined him and declared him too far gone. They quickly returned to the safe haven of their line but the dog did not follow.

With his teeth he began to drag Jack back. He had to avoid shell craters and the odd angry shot but he persevered. Jack's collar tore away so Michael grabbed another part of the coat and continued to drag Jack back. After about two hours Michael could see the French line. The tenacious ambulance dog approached, dragging the critically wounded Marine. A sentry sighted what seemed to be an enemy soldier and was about to shoot when he realised it was Michael dragging a wounded soldier. Two Marines grabbed Jack and carried him to the American dressing station to be assessed.

'Doctor, I think you need to access this one quickly. By the look of his chest he hasn't got long,' the nurse advised.

The female doctor rushed over to examine the young soldier. Not only was he bleeding from his chest wound, he was drowning in his own blood. His face was badly grazed from where Michael had dragged him across the field. He was unrecognisable.

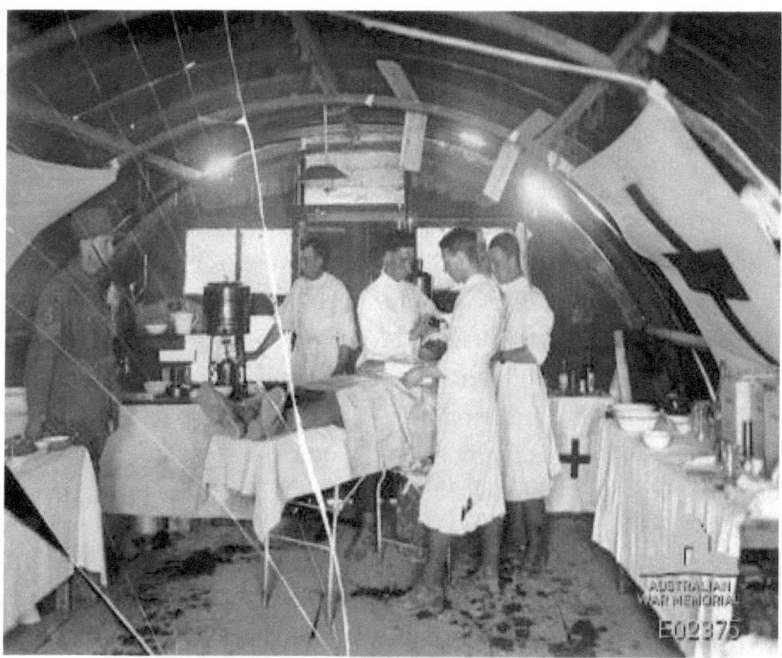

**American Dressing Station**

# 14. Doctor, Doctor

## Pennsylvania 1917

Julie Doherty had been studying at Temple University School of Medicine in Pennsylvania since 1914. She enjoyed the study and the life style and excelled in all her subjects.

She graduated as Dux of the Class and could have chosen any hospital in America to serve her internship. She chose the Western Front in France.

Her brother Jack had been fighting in France since June 1917 and despite receiving letters from him on a regular basis she worried about his welfare. She felt that having come from a military family dating back to the Civil War, she should serve her country.

Julie enlisted as a Medical Officer and sailed to France on 25th November 1917. On the *Carpathia*!

It was a pleasant trip; as an officer she had her own cabin and the seas were smooth. The *Carpathia* docked at Bordeaux on 8th December and she immediately caught the train to the Front.

Dr Doherty was assigned to a dressing station near Cantigny located just behind the Front.

The untried American troops were assigned the task of capturing and holding Cantigny. General Haig saw this as a test for the American fighting spirit.

The Major in charge of the medical team was Steven Duncan, an experienced doctor and formerly Chief Surgeon at John Hopkins in San Francisco.

> 'OK, listen everybody. Tomorrow when this operation commences in earnest there will be many casualties. If any of you have worked in a casualty ward and have experienced the mayhem that quite often occurs, triple that intensity and stress. That will give you some idea about what it's going to be like.
>
> 'Today you should all be checking your instruments, particularly the sharpness of your saws. I am afraid you're going to need them. Nurses make sure there are sufficient bandages and there are sufficient vials of ether and morphine.
>
> 'Good luck everyone and let's all have a drink when it's over.'

Unfortunately the quiet before the storm was cut short; the Germans got wind of the attack and fired fifteen thousand mustard gas shells into the American trenches.

The dressing station received over two hundred and fifty burns patients over a three-hour period. Men with blistering hands, others with blistering skin on their faces, others with blindness. The team rushed to try and give these poor blighters some relief. Julie had never seen anything like it. By the end of the night all patients had been taken by ambulance to the field hospital nearby.

The team were advised to try and get some sleep, as the offensive attack would still be taking place the next morning. Julie collapsed on her stretcher and was asleep in five minutes.

**American Field Hospital France**

# 15.He Ain't Heavy, He's My Brother

Dr Doherty began to examine the soldier; she could determine immediately that he was near death.

'Nurse, clean him up as best you can. I cannot determine the extent of his injuries with so much blood and dirt.'

The young nurse began to wipe the soldier's face, cleaning away the caked blood and grunge.

'Not his face Nurse, his chest!'

Dr Doherty returned to the young soldier. She looked at his battered face and froze. She did not move or utter a word.

'Doctor, are you all right?' asked the nurse.

'He … he's my brother.'

'Oh my God! Well stop staring and save him for goodness' sake.'

The nurse's words prompted Julie into action. She immediately classified him 'priority one'. An ambulance was waiting outside the dressing station within the minute and sped Jack and Julie off to the field hospital five kilometres away.

The first thing Julie organised was a chest X-ray.

At the beginning of the war, chest injuries caused by bullets or shrapnel were bandaged and left to heal, usually resulting in infection and or death. With the advent of X-Rays, doctors behind the front lines were able to locate and remove foreign objects successfully.

Julie was able to determine a piece of shrapnel had penetrated the chest wall puncturing his right lung. If she did not operate immediately he would die within the hour.

She called for two nurses to assist. Only one was available. She requested the help of a senior surgeon. None was available.

Dr Julie Doherty and Nurse Anna Flanagan would have to cope with the resources at their disposal. Nurse Flanagan administered the ether to Jack. Once he was anaesthetised, Julie made a cut down his sternum and spread it wide enough for her to extract the metal from his chest and his right lung. She closed him and immediately called for an ambulance to speed him away to the nearest base hospital where he would be further treated and monitored.

She did not have the luxury of accompanying him, as she was needed back at the dressing station.

> 'My God war is cruel,' she thought as she rode back in the cabin of the ambulance.

Dr Doherty worked another twelve hours: she amputated three legs, two arms, and tried to arrest the bleeding of a young soldier with a severe groin injury – she was unsuccessful, he died.

She tried not to think about Jack but that was an impossible task. When her shift finally ended, she hitched a ride in one of the ambulances going to the base hospital.

Initially, she could not find him. He had been registered as being admitted but he was not in the ward. After asking frantically around the ward she discovered he was undergoing a second operation.

The surgeon, having been told Julie was the patient's sister sought her out.

> 'Are you Jack Doherty's sister?'

> 'I am, Dr. How is he?'

> 'I believe you are also a doctor? The same doctor that performed the first operation?'

> 'Yes.' Julie waited for the castigation.

> 'Well, I can tell you that if you hadn't operated when you did your brother would be dead. There was still some bleeding in the chest cavity but we have been able to stem the flow. Your brother is a very lucky man. My assessment is he will live to fight another day. I would envisage he would be sent to England for his convalescence. Hard to know at this stage for how long.'

> 'That's wonderful doctor. Thank you so much.'

69

'No, thank you – you're the one that saved his life.'

'When do you think I will be able to see him, Dr?'

'I'd leave it until tomorrow.'

'Thank you once again.'

'Stop thanking me. Thank your medical training.'

Julie left the hospital relieved but still concerned. She knew things could still go wrong.

She slept fitfully for four hours before she began her shift again.

Her day was once again filled with amputations and treating burns from mustard gas. She could not stop thinking about Jack and when her shift ended she hitched another ride to the base hospital.

Julie approached Jack's bed slowly. He was asleep. She grabbed a chair and sat next to him, holding his hand. An hour and a half went by and then he opened his eyes. He looked at Julie but his vision was blurred.

'Hello Nurse. Can I have some water please?'

'I'm not a nurse. I'm a doctor, thank you.'

'I'm sorry doctor. I'm not seeing too well at the moment.'

'Yes, that's obvious. You don't even recognise your little sister!'

'Sis! Is that really you?'

'Yes Darling! It's me.'

'How did you know I was here?'

'I brought you here Jack. You came into the dressing station where I was working. I didn't recognise you at first. You were in a right state. I treated you then organised for you to come here.'

'I don't remember what happened to me – one minute I'm running for the Wood and next thing you're sitting beside me.'

'You owe your life to an ambulance dog named Michael. If it wasn't for his persistence and courage you would have died out in no man's land.'

The surgeon who operated on Jack walked up to the bed.

'Well son, you're looking a lot better from when I saw you last. My name is Dr Simmons. I completed the additional surgery on you yesterday. How are you today Dr Doherty?'

'Better for seeing Jack alive, thank you Dr.'

'You owe your life to your sister, young man. If it wasn't for her quick thinking and her skill as a surgeon you wouldn't be here.'

'You operated on me Julie?'

'That's what I'm meant to do Jack. I'm a doctor.'

'Thanks Sis. I can't thank you enough.'

'Enough.'

# 16. In an English Country Garden

**Hatfield House, Hertfordshire**

Jack spent three weeks at the US Military Base Hospital at Neuilly-sur-Seine. Julie visited as much as possible although it proved to be difficult as more and more wounded were being brought into the dressing station.

Jack wrote Julie a note.

Dear Julie,

I have just been informed that I will be transferred to a convalescence hospital in Devon England. I leave tomorrow. It is not much notice so I will understand if you can't see me before I leave.

I know you told me never to mention it again, but I will. Thank you for saving my life Sis – I will never be able to repay the debt.

When this horrid war is over I look forward to seeing you again and sharing Thanksgiving with you, Mom and Gene.

Take care.

All my love

Jack


Julie did not receive the note. The ambulance carrying it was hit by a shell and demolished along with the two ambulance drivers and the three wounded soldiers it was taking to the base hospital.

Julie was looking forward to seeing Jack. It had been four days since her last visit and she was keen to see how he was progressing. She entered his ward only to find his bed occupied by someone else. When she approached the matron and asked where her brother was she was informed of the transfer. Julie knew it would be a long time before she could talk to her big brother again. She felt devastated.

Jack was admitted to Hatfield House in Hertfordshire in August 1918.

Hatfield House was completed in 1611. It was built by Robert Cecil, first Earl of Salisbury and son of Lord Burghley, the Chief Minister of Elizabeth I. The deer park surrounding the house and the older buildings of the Old Palace had been owned by Elizabeth's father, Henry VIII, who had used it as a home for his children: Edward, Elizabeth and Mary. It was while she was living in the Old Palace, in 1558, that Elizabeth learned of her accession to the throne.

The Cecils' former home was at Theobalds, also in Hertfordshire. In 1607, Elizabeth's heir, James I offered to exchange Theobalds for the Old Palace and manor of Hatfield. A draft Parliamentary Act of Exchange survives in the Cecil Papers at Hatfield dated May 1607. Salisbury began building work immediately. The main architect of the house was Robert Lemynge but Simon Basil the Surveyor of the King's Works, and Inigo Jones also contributed to the design.

Salisbury had been appointed Lord Treasurer in April 1607 as well as Chief Secretary, but he became ill and died, aged just 48, in April 1612. Although he was buried at Hatfield, he didn't live to enjoy the house that was to become the home of his descendants, the Cecils, for the next 400 years.

Hatfield was now home to one hundred and fifty convalescing soldiers who had access to the magnificent gardens and the extensive deer park. Most of these men were either in wheelchairs or walking with the aid of crutches.

Jack could walk unaided but still suffered from terrible chest pains. He made some lifelong friends during his sojourn at Hatfield, including his roommate Captain Gregory Mathers. They were both a long way from home yet they had both been raised in the Chesapeake area. Their family homes were only one mile apart yet they had never met before sharing a room at Hatfield.

The two men would walk through the gardens discussing all manner of things including the war. Neither of them had any regrets about their choice of career, despite their injuries.

Jack stayed at Hatfield for two months and at the end of his time there was almost fully recovered. He had been writing regularly to his mother and his sister assuring them of his recovery and his imminent return to the front.

# 17. You're Going Home Soldier

Jack was walking in the deer park with Greg when they were approached by a Lieutenant.

'Which one of you soldiers is Captain Doherty?'

'I am.'

'You have immediate orders to leave Hatfield at once.' He handed Jack an envelope.

'So, I'm back in the fray?'

'I'm afraid not Captain. You are being sent home to the good old USA.'

'No, surely not! I'm probably fitter than most of the doughboys over there fighting at the moment.'

'That may well be the case but orders are orders. I am instructed to escort you to London to board a ship to take you home. Now please excuse us, Captain Mathers. We need to pack the Captain's bags and get to London.'

'When am I departing, sir?'

'Tomorrow morning.'

Jack was unaware that his stepfather Rear Admiral Eugene Leutze had, at the behest of Jack's mother Lucy, pulled a few strings with his contacts in the Marines. She wanted her son out of harm's way – she had lost a husband; she wasn't going to lose a son.

Jack packed his suitcase and said farewell to the nursing staff who had looked after him so well. The Lieutenant had arrived in a black Cadillac with a driver at the wheel. It only took them ninety minutes to make the trip to Southampton. Jack was booked into the historic Dolphin Hotel.

After a restless night he went down to the hotel restaurant and enjoyed a hearty breakfast of eggs and bacon. He had just completed his meal when the officer who had escorted him entered the room.

'How was breakfast, Captain?'

'Very good! The best I've had for a while as you can imagine.'

'Good-oh. Well, it's time to go. Fetch your bag and I'll fix up the bill.'

They both got onto the Army vehicle and drove to the dock just two miles away.

'Well, there she is. The ship that's taking you home.'

Jack stared. He couldn't believe it: The ship that was taking him home was the *Carpathia*.

The same ship that had saved his mother, sister and himself when the *Titanic* sank; the same ship that had transported him to France to join the great fray. Now the same ship would take him home.

He boarded his old friend and was shown to his cabin by an orderly. There was no need for any instructions – he knew where everything was. He heard the ship's horn signalling their imminent departure and decided to go up to the main deck and wave goodbye to England. The ship pulled away from the dock with the aid of three tugs – they were on their way.

The *Carpathia* was about eight hours into the journey sailing through the Celtic Sea Jack was sitting at a table in the dining room talking to some American passengers about what life had been like back home during these tumultuous times.

Suddenly, they heard a huge boom and the ship rocked violently.

'We've been hit! Quick! Everybody to the lifeboats!' Jack yelled. He knew the drill; he'd been there before.

The Imperial German Navy submarine *U-55* had torpedoed her. Of three torpedoes fired at the ship, one impacted the port side while the other penetrated the engine room, killing two firemen and three trimmers. As *Carpathia* began to settle by the head and list to port, Captain William Prothero gave the order to abandon ship. All fifty-seven passengers and two hundred and eighteen surviving crewmembers boarded the lifeboats as the vessel sank.

A British ship, the HMS *Snowdrop*, a small Azalea-class sloop, rescued all the passengers and surviving crew. Jack had been in this situation before. He'd prayed never again.

The *Snowdrop* transported the survivors to the port of Liverpool. The RMS *Cedric* then took the passengers to Boston. They only lost a week from their original schedule.

Jack's mother Lucy and her husband Gene were at the wharf to greet him.

> 'Jack you look wonderful! I was expecting you in a wheelchair or something. Here you are in your Marine's uniform looking every bit the returning hero.'

> 'Thanks Mom, I'm OK. Certainly not an invalid. Though the doctors tell me I have to take it easy for a while.'

> 'It looks like they've given you a promotion Jack. Captain – that's pretty impressive.' Gene smiled proudly at him.

> 'Thanks, sir. Yes, I was promoted in the field to First Lieutenant then I got promoted again after I was wounded.'

> 'Well, we better get on our way if we are going to make it back to Washington by nightfall.'

The three of them were driven in the Admiral's car back to Washington DC, a seven-hour drive.

Lucy tried to get Jack to talk about his experiences in the war but Jack proved very reluctant to divulge any real detail. He did tell them about his close friend John being killed.

On arrival they had a light meal prepared by the housemaid and then all three retired for the evening. It had been a big day.

Over the next few weeks Jack spent his time walking around the capital visiting various monuments and contemplating his future.

He spent a week with an old school friend in his family's Chesapeake Bay holiday cabin, which reminded him of his childhood living on the shore with his mother, father and sister.

The time arrived when he was due to present himself to Marine Corps Base Quantico for duty. The base was only forty miles from Washington DC so visiting his mother would be relatively easy.

Jack had made the decision to remain in the Marines and that is where he would carve out a career. His commander, Colonel James Pickering earmarked Jack for bigger and greater things. Jack was enrolled and completed a number of courses, which would further his career.

# 18. What Are You Doing After the War?

# 11th November 1918

**Armistice Day London**

**Armistice Day on the Western Front**

The final Allied push towards the German border began on 17th October 1918. As the British, French and American armies advanced, the alliance between the Central Powers began to collapse. Turkey signed an armistice at the end of October, Austria-Hungary followed on 3rd November.

Germany began to crumble from within. Faced with the prospect of returning to sea, the sailors of the High Seas Fleet stationed at Kiel mutinied on 29th October. Within a few days, the entire city was in their control and the revolution spread throughout the country. On 9th November the Kaiser abdicated, slipping across the border into the Netherlands, and exile. A German Republic was declared and an offer of peace was extended to the Allies. At 5 am on the morning of 11th November an armistice was signed in a train carriage parked in a French forest near the front lines.

The terms of the agreement called for the cessation of fighting along the entire Western Front, to begin at precisely 11 am that morning. After more than four years of bloody conflict, the Great War was at an end.

Colonel Thomas Gowenlock served as an intelligence officer in the American 1st Division. He was on the front line that November morning and wrote of his experience a few years later:

> On the morning of November 11th, I sat in my dugout in Le Gros Faux, which was again our Division HQ, talking to our Chief of Staff, Colonel John Greely, and Lieutenant Colonel Paul Peabody, our G-1. A signal corps officer entered and handed us the following message:

Official Radio from Paris - 6:01 A.M., Nov. 11th, 1918. Marshal Foch to the Commander-in-Chief.

1. Hostilities will cease on the entire Front beginning at 11 o'clock, November 11th (French hour).

2. The Allied troops will not go beyond the line reached at that hour on that date until further orders.

MARSHAL FOCH

5:45 A.M.

'Well, fini la guerre!' said Colonel Greely.

'Sure looks like it,' I agreed.

'Do you know what I want to do now?' he said. 'I'd like to get on one of those little horse-drawn canal boats in southern France and lie in the sun the rest of my life.'

My watch said nine o'clock. With only two hours to go, I drove over to the bank of the Meuse River to see the finish. The shelling was heavy and, as I walked down the road, it grew steadily worse. It seemed to me that every battery in the world was trying to burn up its guns. At last eleven o'clock came – but the firing continued. The men on both sides had decided to give each other all they had – their farewell to arms. It was a very natural impulse after their years of war, but unfortunately many fell after eleven o'clock that day.


All over the world on 11th November 1918, people were celebrating, dancing in the streets, drinking champagne, and hailing the Armistice that meant the end of the war. But at the front there was no celebration. Many soldiers believed the Armistice only a temporary measure and that the war would soon go on. As night came, the quietness, unearthly in its penetration, began to eat into their souls. The men sat around log fires, the first they had ever had at the Front. They were trying to reassure themselves that there were no enemy batteries spying on them from the next hill and no German bombing planes approaching to blast them out of existence. They talked in low tones. They were nervous.

After the long months of intense strain, of keying themselves up to the daily mortal danger, of thinking always in terms of war and the enemy, the abrupt release from it all was physical and psychological agony. Some suffered a total nervous collapse. Some, of a steadier temperament, began to hope they would some day return to home and the embrace of loved ones. Some could think only of the crude little crosses that marked the graves of their comrades. Some fell into an exhausted sleep. All were bewildered by the sudden meaninglessness of their existence as soldiers – and through their teeming memories paraded that swiftly moving cavalcade of Cantigny, Soissons, St Mihiel, the Meuse-Argonne and Sedan.

What was to come next? They did not know – and hardly cared. Their minds were numbed by the shock of peace. The past consumed their whole consciousness. The present did not exist. And the future was inconceivable.

# 19. War's End for Augustin

Augustin Trébuchon was a normal young lad, although his childhood was anything but normal. His mother died when he was eight and he and his four younger brothers and sisters were raised by their father Joseph, in the French village of Montchabrier in the Lozère.

The Lozère region is very mountainous and young Augustin enjoyed running up the steep slopes and descending at full pace.

Joseph died when Augustin was just seventeen and the youngest sister was twelve. It was decided by the village priest that the four young children should be sent to orphanages leaving Augustine alone. He remained in the family home. He never married and was a communal shepherd tending his sheep in the beloved mountain slopes. He played accordion at village marriages before volunteering for the army on 4<sup>th</sup> August 1914.

He joined the 415<sup>th</sup> Infantry Regiment as a messenger. He had already served in the second battle of the Marne and at Verdun, Artois and the Somme before arriving in the Ardennes near the end of the war. He had twice been wounded, including a bad injury to his left arm from an exploding shell. Augustin was promoted to the rank of *Soldat de Première Classe* (Private First Class) in September 1918. His commanding officer said he was ''a good soldier having always achieved his duty, of remarkable calm, setting the best example to his young comrades'.'

On the 11<sup>th</sup> November he was summoned to his commanding officer's headquarters and given an envelope.

> 'Private, this message will inform the commander of the 163<sup>rd</sup> Infantry that the armistice will take effect at precisely 11a.m. today. It is imperative you get this message through. We don't want any more French blood spilt on this God-forsaken battlefield.'

At Vrigne-sur-Meuse, in the Ardennes, the 163<sup>rd</sup> Infantry Division was ordered to attack an elite German unit, the 'Hannetons'. General Henri Gouraud told his men to cross the Meuse River and to attack 'as fast as possible, by whatever means and regardless of cost'.

It has been speculated that the attack was to end any possible hesitation or doubts by German negotiators at Compiègne. General Foch, the French commander, believed the Germans were reluctant to sign and so ordered Général Philippe Pétain to press on across the Meuse River.

Trébuchon was halfway between Sedan and Charleville-Mézières. Rain was falling and the Meuse was flooding. Its width was put at seventy metres. The temperature was well below freezing. Warfare had destroyed bridges across the river and sappers worked by night and in fog to build a plank footbridge across a lock. There had been no reconnaissance of the other bank because bad weather had kept the spotter plane on the ground. Around seven hundred men crossed the river a little after 8 am, taking a telephone wire with them. Some fell in the river and the first deaths of the battle were by drowning.

The fog cleared at 10.30 am and the French could see the German positions a little higher up, a few hundred metres away. The French were spread over three kilometres between the Meuse and a railway line. The Germans opened fire with machine guns. The French sent up a spotter plane now that the fog had lifted and the artillery on the other bank could open fire without fear of killing their own. Darkness fell at 6 pm and the battle continued until news of the Armistice arrived.

The last of the ninety-one French soldiers to die after 11th November was Augustin Trébuchon – he was 40 years old. He fell near the railway line with his message still in his hand.

The Armistice followed and the French withdrew without honouring their dead. Ninety-one brave French soldiers were left in the mud and slime, never to be buried with full honours. They all died after the war had ended. Augustin was named as the last French casualty of the war.

**Augustin Trébuchon**

# 20. War's End for Dr Julie Doherty

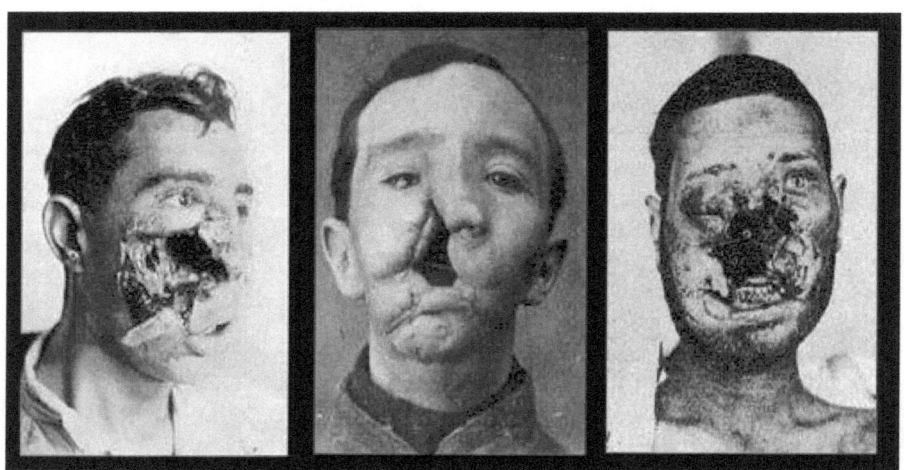

Dr Julie Doherty had been working 'full tilt' at the field base hospital on the Front since the beginning of June 1918. Apart from saving her brother Jack's life she had saved many more young Doughboy's' lives. She had been horrified at the injuries she encountered, particularly the facial injuries. These young men would return home only to find civilians looking away in horror, or crossing quickly to the other side of the street.

She decided that when the end of the war finally came, she would move to Britain and accept the offer to study plastic surgery under Dr Harold Gillies at the Queen's Hospital in Sidcup, Kent. Dr Gillies was pleased to have Julie as an assistant and together they performed some eleven thousand operations at the Queen's Hospital between 1917 and 1925.

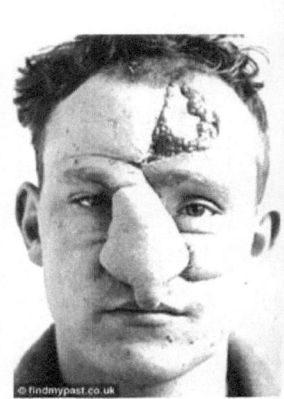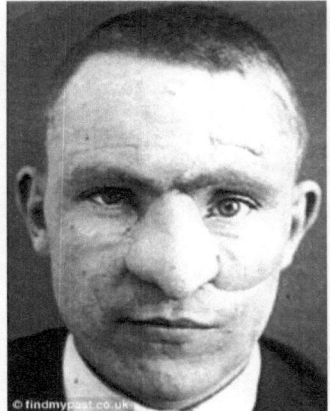

**The photos above show the progress of surgery performed by Dr Gillies assisted by Dr Doherty.**

Julie enjoyed her time at the Queen's Hospital under the guidance of Dr Gillies. She also enjoyed living in Kent which was often described as the garden of England. Julie also enjoyed visiting France when she had time off she took the ferry from Dover to Calais. Although her time in France was horrendous during the war she appreciated the beauty of the country when on leave. Paris was her favourite city in the world.

Julie discovered golf while living in England. She joined the Royal Blackheath Golf Club and began having Julie discovered golf while living in England; she joined the Royal Blackheath Golf Club and began having lessons. After a year of playing most weekends she had reduced her handicap to eighteen. The other lady golfers were most impressed and invited her to play pennants for the club.

In the spring of 1922 she played in a mixed foursome competing against a couple from the Grove Golf Club visiting from Hertfordshire. Her partner was the club captain, Anthony Pittard – he played off ten and Julie was now down to fifteen.

Their opponents were Dr Harry de Neville and Sandra Scott. Harry was a very handsome, athletic-looking man who had also been a medico in the war and, as it turned out, he shared her interest in plastic surgery. Sandra had been a nurse in France and had worked with Harry.

The round went Julie's and Tony's way; they won two up with one to play.

'Well everybody, bloody good game! 'Let's retire to the club house for a stiff drink,' suggested Tony.

'Sounds good to me.' Harry agreed. 'I hope you ladies will join us.'

'Yes, of course. I think we both need it,' said Julie.

Away from the competitive environment of the golf course the four loosened up and were chatting away.

'Julie, are you in General Practice?' asked Harry.

'No, I'm working with Dr Harold Gillies at the Queen's Hospital. You may have heard of him?'

'Heard of him! My God! He is the father of plastic surgery. That is also my speciality although you wouldn't mention my name in the same sentence as his'.

'I have been working under his guidance now for three and a half years. He has taught me so much.'

'That really is impressive Julie. Well done.'

'I think I was just fortunate that Dr Gillies took me under his wing.'

The day ended and all went their separate ways. The losing team headed back up to Hertfordshire and Julie and Tony headed home.

# 21. Turning British

Julie arrived home after a particularly intense day completing three skin grafts and a partial nose reconstruction. She collapsed into her favourite wingback chair with a Scotch and water in hand. Her eyelids became heavy and she felt herself starting to doze off when the telephone on the small round table next to her started to ring, startling her out of her comatose state.

'Dr Doherty speaking.'

'Hello Julie, it's Harry. Dr Harry de Neville.'

'Oh, hello Harry. How are you?'

'I'm fine. And you?'

'Yes. Yes, I'm fine.' Julie wondered why Harry was calling her.

'I hope you don't mind me calling you at home but I have something rather important to ask you.'

'Really, what is it?'

'Well, I'm not very good at this sort of thing.'

'Sorry? What sort of thing, Harry?'

'Asking a beautiful young woman out to lunch.'

'Is that why you called me? Interrupting my Scotch after a very busy day in surgery?

'I'm afraid so. Sorry.'

'I'd love to. Where are you taking me?'

'Oh splendid! Well ... I thought Claridges.'

'Wonderful! When?'

'When? Oh of course ... When? Well, I thought this coming Sunday, if that's convenient for you.'

'Yes, Sunday would be fine. What time will you pick me up?'

Let's say eleven? That should give us plenty of time to get into London, park etc.'

'Lovely! See you on Sunday at eleven.'

'Excellent! I am looking forward to it. Goodbye.'

'Goodbye.'

Julie returned the handset to its cradle. She smiled to herself thinking how nice it would be having lunch at Claridges with Harry. She had often thought of him after the golf game – what a catch he would be! A handsome young plastic surgeon who came from a very well to do family.

She had five days to decide what she would wear, only five days.

At last Sunday arrived and Harry pulled up in his Rolls Royce Phantom. She had never seen such a magnificent motor vehicle.

**1925 Rolls Royce Phantom**

The trip to Pall Mall London only took forty-five minutes. The time was taken up by idle chat about golf and the beauty of the countryside.

Harry pulled up outside the famous hotel and handed the keys to the white-gloved parking attendant. Parking such a prestigious car was second nature to the Claridges attendants. The doorman opened the door for the handsome young couple and they proceeded to 'The Foyer Restaurant'.

Once seated, they spoke about this and that, nothing too heavy. It wasn't until the main course, *Filet Mignon*, was served that Harry began the conversation that had really been on his mind.

'Julie, I have as you know been working in the field of plastic surgery since the war ended and have decided that this is the field of medicine I wish to specialise in for the foreseeable future. I was wondering if you would introduce me to Dr Gillies on the basis that I become an intern as it were under his tutelage.'

'I see, so that is the reason for this luncheon invitation. Not because you were attracted to me or found my conversation interesting. All you wanted was an introduction to my boss in the hope that knowing me might hold some sway.'

'Now Julie, don't get me wrong! I am attracted to you, very much. It's just that seeing you already work under his wing ... well, you know what I mean?'

'No, I don't know what you mean. Is it my feminine wiles or my intellect? Or where I work that attracts you to me?'

'Julie!'

'Don't Julie me Harry! I would like you to take me home.'

'But you haven't eaten your lunch yet!'

'I've lost my appetite. Please take me home!'

They left the restaurant. The drive home was in silence, completely different from the trip to London.

Harry pulled up outside her cottage. Julie got out and not looking back, opened the front door and disappeared.

Harry knew he had his work cut out.

# 22.Forgive Me

*'A mistake is always forgivable, rarely excusable and always unacceptable.'*

*Robert Fripp*

Julie was in her office at the Queen's Hospital checking the photographic results from some recent operations she had completed.

'Excuse me Dr Doherty, these flowers have been delivered for you. Where would you like me to place them?' The orderly was holding a large bouquet.

Julie got up from her desk and opened the card attached to the magnificent display of red roses.

'In the ward where you feel they would be best appreciated thank you.'

The orderly looked puzzled but nevertheless took the flowers away.

The next day a similar delivery was attempted. This time the three dozen roses were white. She read the card and again sent them away.

Every day for a fortnight roses of different colours were delivered and distributed amongst the wards. The patients thought they were wonderful but Julie was not impressed.

Harry thought he'd better try a different tactic.

It was Sunday the 6<sup>th</sup> June 1926 and Julie had just arrived home from golf. She packed her clubs away and was ready for her whisky. The front door bell rang.

'Who could this be?' she thought. 'On a Sunday afternoon. Hope it's not a call out to the hospital.'

She answered the door only to find Harry.

Annoyed, she demanded, 'What do you want?'

'I know I acted terribly Julie. But believe me, the last thing I wanted to do was offend you.'

'Is that it?'

'No it isn't. Please ... I was ... I still am ... very attracted to you. My reason for asking about the position at Queens was to be near you. Disbelieve that if you like but I am telling you the truth.'

Julie said nothing as she thought about all the roses he had sent. Perhaps she had been a bit harsh. 'Come in.'

Harry entered the small cottage and was shown into the living area.

'Julie, I have been distraught since the other Sunday. I really have.'

'Guess I'll take your word for it, Harry.'

'Thank you.'

'I was just about to pour myself a Scotch. Would you like to join me?'

'Yes, I would. Thank you.'

After some awkward small talk Harry brought up the real reason for his visit. This time it had nothing to do with his future career.

'Julie, do you enjoy opera?'

'Yes, I do. Well, not all opera. But most. Why do you ask?'

'I was wondering if you would accompany me to Dame Nellie Melba's farewell concert. It's this coming Tuesday. I've got tickets in the box next to the Royal Box.'

'Goodness me! I don't know if I should.

'Of course you should. The King and Queen will be our neighbours. Besides, Nellie is going back to Australia soon. We'll probably never have the opportunity to see her again.'

'You're right. Yes. I would love to go.'

'Wonderful, it's at the Royal Opera House at Covent Garden. I will pick you up at seven.'

With that Harry got up and left, feeling pretty pleased with himself. Mission accomplished.

ROYAL OPERA
COVENT GARDEN
(Proprietors - The Grand Opera Syndicate, Ltd.)

Under the Patronage and in the Presence of
THEIR MAJESTIES THE KING AND QUEEN

Farewell Appearance of

Dame

# NELLIE MELBA

IN OPERA

AT

COVENT GARDEN

Tuesday, June 8th, 1926

# Tuesday 8th June 1926

It was a beautiful summer's evening; Harry enjoyed the trip down to Kent in the Phantom. He arrived at Julie's cottage at 6.55 pm – he wasn't going to be late.

He rang the bell. Julie opened the front door and standing before her was Harry, resplendent in a Savile Row dinner suit. Julie was dressed in a flowing red evening gown, with a string of rubies around her neck. She looked beautiful.

They both complimented each other then began the drive to Covent Garden. The conversation was more relaxed. Julie knew she had made the right decision.

Harry parked in front of the Opera House and helped Julie alight from the motor vehicle. An attendant drove the Phantom and parked at the back of the complex.

As they entered the Opera House they were astounded to see how many people were there. Dame Nellie was certainly popular and would be sorely missed.

Harry and Julie were shown to their box. Harry had not exaggerated – they were right next to the Royal Box. Without being too obvious, they could get a glimpse of the chairs where the King and Queen would be seated when they arrived.

There was excitement and tension in the air. This truly was a special occasion – not only the final concert for the greatest of divas but the King and Queen attending to say goodbye to the much-loved Dame Nellie Melba.

At 8 pm the royal party arrived and were escorted to their box. Five minutes later the curtain rose to thunderous applause.

Dame Nellie had chosen her favourite opera *La Bohème* for her final performance in Britain. Mimi was regarded as her finest role.

Puccini's love story, set in the Latin quarter of Paris around 1830, was always going to be Melba's farewell concert. Mimi, a consumptive dressmaker, falls in love with Rodolfo, a poor student and eventually dies in his arms.

At the conclusion of what could be argued as her finest performance the audience rose to their feet applauding without respite for a full twenty minutes. The stage was covered in flowers, which were later collected and sent to a London war veteran's' home on Melba's instruction.

King George and Queen Elizabeth invited Nellie to the Royal Box where they enthusiastically congratulated her, not only for the night's performance but also for a wonderful career.

Dame Nellie left the Royal Box and entered Harry's and Julie's box, much to Julie's surprise and astonishment.

'Hello Harry, how are you?'

'I'm well Ma'am. All the better for having the opportunity of hearing you sing again. I am only sorry it may be the last time.'

'Are you going to introduce me to your partner?'

'Oh, sorry! But of course. Dame Nellie Melba, may I introduce you to my good friend Dr Julie Doherty.'

'Another doctor in the house! I feel positively healthy, thank you.'

'Yes, Ma'am. You certainly look healthy to me.'

'How are your parents Harry? Last time I saw them was when I spent a weekend up at the castle.'

'They're very well Dame Nellie. I will pass on your regards.'

'Please do. Well I must go back stage and say hello. Or perhaps that should be 'good-bye' to some well-wishers. Good-bye Harry. And good-bye Julie. It was a pleasure to meet you.'

'Good bye Ma'am. May you have a wonderful life back home in Australia.'

'Thank you. I'm sure I will'.

Julie was still astonished. 'So?'

'So what?'

'How do you know Dame Nellie Melba?'

'My parents are patrons of the opera. They've had a lot to do with her over the years. In fact, my mother was the first person to recognise her immense talent when she first arrived in England.'

'Who exactly are your parents Harry?' Julie realised she hadn't a clue.

'They are the Earl and Duchess of Westmoreland. I'm sorry, I thought you may have known.'

'No. To tell you the truth, I hadn't thought about it.'

Harry and Julie returned to Claridges for a late night supper and then drove back to Julie's cottage.

'Thank you Harry. That was the best night of my life. I don't know how to thank you.'

Harry could think of a way but thought better of it. He kissed Julie lightly on the lips and bade her farewell.

Driving back to Hertfordshire Harry's thoughts drifted back and forth from the evening they had just enjoyed to how much he liked Julie. He hoped this night would develop into a meaningful relationship in the future.

It would.

# 23. Do You Take This Doctor?

The relationship between Harry and Julie started to blossom. They not only played golf on a regular basis but they became a part of the elite London social scene. They were regular theatre-goers, enjoying stage shows at the Palladium as well as operas at Covent Garden.

Harry never mentioned transferring to Queens again, or working with Dr Harold Gillies.

## 24<sup>th</sup> December 1928

Harry invited Julie to celebrate Christmas with his family at his parents' home, Raby Castle, near Staindrop in County Durham. She had met the Earl and Duchess a number of times but had never visited the ancestral home. This was the time of year where she really missed her family, so to be with Harry and his family was a real treat.

The drive to Durham took them the best part of the day and it was 5 pm when they drove up the long tree lined driveway. Julie was awestruck – this was not just a home, it was a medieval castle!

### Raby Castle

'My God! Harry, it is huge! When was it built?'

'Between 1367 and 1390 we believe.'

'Has it been in your family all this time?'

'Pretty much. In 1378 Thomas Hatfield, Bishop of Durham, granted John de Neville a licence to fortify his property at Raby. John died in 1388 and was succeeded by his son, Ralph. Almost nothing of our family's papers survived this period so there is little documentary evidence of Raby Castle's construction. Ralph, my ancestor, was created Earl of Westmoreland on 29th September, 1397 by Richard II as a reward for his loyalty in the face of political unrest.'

'How large are the grounds?'

'Two hundred acres.'

'I can see the deer. Are there many living here?'

'I'm not sure how many. But yes, plenty of red deer and fallows.'

'Beautiful, just beautiful. You are very lucky Harry.'

'Yes, I suppose I am. But I'd give it all up just to hear you say "yes".'

'What ever do you mean?'

'I mean: will you marry me Julie?'

'Oh my God, Harry! This is a surprise. Straight out of the blue.'

Harry took a small box from his jacket pocket and opened it. Inside was a ring with a large cornflower-blue sapphire set with one-carat diamonds on either side.

'Oh Harry, it's beautiful. Stunning.'

'Well, my love? What's your answer?'

'Yes! Of course ... Yes!'

They embraced in the front seat of the Rolls overlooking the magnificent estate. This was how they began their new lives together.

'Well. I suppose we should go and inform your parents.'

'They already know.'

'They do? You've told them? Before you actually asked me?'

'Don't be upset Julie. I was obligated to tell them.'

'Obligated?'

'It's a family law, an age old tradition. When the first-born son intends to marry he must get permission from his parents.'

'What if they don't approve?'

'If he insists on marrying the one he loves against his parents wishes, he loses all his ancestral rights.'

'I assume your parents approved of me?'

'They were concerned you weren't English. You know ... English bloodlines etc.'

'So they didn't want their son to marry a brash American?'

'Julie, I told them I was more than willing to walk away from my inheritance if that's what it took. They backed down. They really like you and will learn to love you. It will just take a little time.'

'Harry, you were willing to lose this castle and the rest of your family's wealth plus your title when your father dies – for me?'

'Absolutely, without a second thought. You are the most important thing in my life, you always will be.'

They embraced again and continued their trip up the tree-lined driveway where they were greeted by the Earl and Duchess.

'Congratulations you two.' The Earl greeted them warmly.

'Yes, my dears, we are both very happy for you,' agreed the Duchess.

'Well you are doing your bit for international relations or should I say international relationships.' Harry's father looked pleased.

All four laughed and headed into the castle for tea and scones.

A servant brought them tea on a beautiful mahogany tea trolley

'Now Julie, we know very little about your family. Since we are going to be related – so to speak – we'd love to hear your story.' The Duchess began to pour the tea.

Julie paused for a moment and then began her story. She told them about her father going down with the *Titanic* and how her brother, mother and she were saved. She explained that her mother remarried and was now the wife of a US Rear Admiral; her brother Jack was a Major in the Marines stationed near Washington. Jack's parents listened intently until she had finished.

'So, that's an amazing family you've got there Julie. Obviously the military has played a significant part.'

'It certainly has, sir. Also considering I was an Army doctor in France and Belgium during the war.'

The next day they celebrated Christmas with Harry's two brothers and their wives and an assortment of dignitaries from the area.

Julie and Harry departed on Boxing Day planning their wedding at the castle on the trip home. They had decided they would be married in July, barely seven months away.

Julie telephoned her mother in Washington to break the news. Her mother was delighted and without discussing it with her husband, committed to being there in July. She also telephoned Jack. He was happy for her and assured Julie he would be able to get leave to attend.

# July 1929

Raby Castle had never looked better. There were white ribbons tied to the trees lining the driveway and the grounds had been prepared as for a royal visit. The grand dining room was decorated in white and was waiting for the four hundred guests to arrive.

Everything went well and the married couple left at midnight. The following day they were driven by Harry's father's chauffeur to the shipping port of Sunderland. Harry had booked a six-week cruise to the Far East visiting Singapore, Hong Kong, and Shanghai and back via Malaya. Neither of them had been to any of these destinations and they were both looking forward to a cruise of discovery.

They boarded the *Empress of Britain* and were shown to their cabin which was of course first class. This was going to be an experience that would change their lives forever.

**Empress of Britain**

# 24.War's End for Captain Jack Doherty

Jack enjoyed his time at Marine Corps Base Quantico. He excelled in the courses he undertook including learning Mandarin.

In 1920 he was transferred to China, a country he found intriguing. Following World War I, and as a result of the decline of military forces in Peking, the Marines maintained the largest Legation Guard presence in the city, even larger than the Japanese.

Jack requested he be transferred to the Mounted Unit. He loved horses and thought it would probably be the only opportunity he would have to be in a cavalry regiment. His request was granted and consequently he rode with 'the finest men and horses in the US Marines'.

# 1922

As a result of fighting near Peking between Warlords Wu Pei-fu of Shangtung and Chang Tso-Lin of Manchuria, the Marines sealed their portion of the Legation Quarter. Furthermore, Marines opened fire from the Tartar Wall on rebel soldiers attempting to use a ram on the Chien Men Gate.

Jack was regarded as a sharpshooter and managed to down several of the rebels before they fled.

The following month one hundred and fifty US Marines from the USS *Huron* landed at Tientsin in response to fighting between Gen Wu Pei fu and Gen Chang Tso-lin's troops, also near Peking. They remained for several days in case they were needed. The Marine Legation Guard grew to a strength of five hundred and twenty-five.

Jack received another promotion: he was now Major Jack Doherty.

The young Major was summoned back to Washington in December 1923, for what reason he wasn't sure. He sailed home on the USS *Augusta*, one of the most powerful battle ships in the fleet.

Jack was posted to several Marine Corp installations over the next nine years including:

Marine Corps Base Camp Pendleton

Oceanside, California

Marine Corps Logistics Base Albany

Albany, Georgia

Marine Corps Base Camp Lejeune

Jacksonville, North Carolina

Marine Barracks, Washington, DC

Washington, DC

Camp H. M. Smith, Marine Corps Base Hawaii

Aiea, Hawaii

In that time he had received a number of promotions and by 1932 he was a Brigadier General in the Marine Corps.

He had married and had two boys, Tom and Peter, now aged ten and eight. Life was good, although he did get frustrated not being able to use his skills and experience in peacetime. He had however, gained an enormous amount of experience and training in 'intelligence' and those skills can be used anytime; peace or war.

# 25.Like Father, Like Son

## Washington DC 1932

Jack took the same route as his father took back in 1910, along side the Anacostia River. The walk would take him to the Washington Naval Yard where he had been summoned to meet with Eugene Leutze, Under Secretary of the Navy. The former Admiral was effectively his stepfather, although neither of them really saw it that way.

Jack waited in the waiting room trying to anticipate why he had been summoned to this meeting.

'Come on in Jack.' The Under Secretary rarely greeted his subordinates this way but Jack shared Thanksgiving and Christmas with him each year. They were close.

'Take a seat Jack. Can I get Nancy to get you a coffee?'

'No thank you, sir. I'm fine for now.'

'Right, down to business. Jack, as you know Europe is still a hot bed. If there's going to be another war it will be there. The President is concerned that this fellow Hitler intends to rip up the Treaty of Versailles and start building a military force.'

'Yes sir, I agree it should be cause for concern.'

'Good. Which brings me to why I called you here today. We – I mean the President and I – feel we need a strong diplomatic presence in Berlin. We need *you* there, Jack. Your orders are to transfer to the American Embassy where you will be the senior military officer. You will report directly to me. Our Ambassador William Dodd has informed us that life in Berlin is quite safe, although there has been some unrest relating to the Nazis' treatment of the Jews and the Communists. I don't think it's particularly serious at the moment. There is an American School for the boys, but if it were me, I'd board them back here in Washington.'

'When am I expected to be in Berlin, sir?'

'The 1$^{st}$ of March.'

'That doesn't give me a lot of time to get organised. Nevertheless, we'll be there.'

'Well done! How do you think Anna is going to take it, Jack?'

'She's a Marine's wife. We've had a few postings around the States. She'll be OK'.

Jack returned to his family home and broke the news. Surprisingly they all took it in their stride.

The two boys, Tom and Peter were enrolled as boarders in St Alban's School. Jack and Anna flew from Norfolk, Virginia, to Germany via Bermuda and the Azores. They landed in Berlin on 1st March 1932. The American Ambassador, William Dodd met them at the newly constructed airport. It was decided that the Dohertys should live inside the American compound. The two-bed bungalow was beautifully decorated and was more than adequate for their needs.

The first thing Jack requested was a full briefing by Ambassador Dodd on the situation and what effect Germany's military ambitions were having on the rest of Europe.

Jack walked into William Dodd's office on 7th March fully prepared for a detailed briefing. He got it.

'Well Brigadier General I will reiterate what I have been telling Washington. Please stop me if you have any questions.'

'Thank you sir. Please call me Jack.'

'OK Jack. And likewise. Call me Bill.'

'Let's begin with my assessment of Hitler's political future. I should go back a couple of years so you can appreciate where he has come from and where he's heading.

'Hitler's political movement, which was practically down and out following the abortive *putsch* in Munich in 1923, has since gained a large ascendency with the increase of unemployment in Germany. The past year, particularly, has witnessed a phenomenal gain in successive local elections, the Nazis having profited tremendously by the depression. My belief is that there is no limit to future Nazi gains and that they will continue a geometric progression.

'The results of the general election in September 1930 showed that the Nazis achieved eighteen percent of the popular vote. This result showed that Hitler's gains were made mostly at the expense of the non-Socialist parties of the middle and the right. Hitler, however has not been unable to decrease the vote of the two Catholic parties – the Bavarian People's Party and Centre Party – or to affect the combined strength of the Socialist parties of the Left, that is the Communists and Social-Democrats.

'The most significant local election during 1931 was that of the Free State of Hesse. Unlike the other local elections, it had more than local significance. The distribution of political strength in Hesse resembles more closely the political constellation throughout the Reich. If the results of the local elections were replicated in a general election, the Catholic parties would obtain about fifteen per cent, the non-Socialist parties fifteen per cent, the Marxist parties of the Left about thirty five per cent, and the Nazis thirty five per cent. The Nazis would certainly become the strongest party in a new Reichstag. Hitler's claims that he could get fifty percent of the popular vote enabling the Nazis to govern alone in their own right seems at this stage improbable.

'However, there is a strong possibility that if he fails to get the numbers to govern alone he could enter a coalition with the two Catholic parties, giving him Government.'

Jack listened carefully. 'Just one question Bill. Could the other minority parties enter an agreement which would stymie Hitler's ambitions?'

'They could, but very unlikely. They are diametrically opposed on pretty well every issue.'

'I see. Please continue.'

'Hitler's interview with the foreign press, on December 4th, in which he stressed his capitalistic program assuming the sanctity of private foreign debts, has, according to his own lieutenants, cooled the ardour of many of the more radical elements within the National-Socialist Party.

'However, while it has allayed their fears, it has failed to attract to his cause influential citizens. The prominent Germans who are Hitler followers can be counted on one hand, although a few rich industrialists would be included. The recent assurances in Hitler's speeches on economic matters have won over certain business elements but have alienated the radical youth who were the building blocks for the movement. As the latter far outnumber the former from a voting standpoint it is felt in most circles that Nazi gains in voting strength will be considerably diminished in the immediate future.'

'May I interrupt you again? How closely is the Nazis' manifesto aligned to the Fascists in Italy?'

'The program of Fascist Italy really has little in common with that of the Nazis in Germany. Whereas Fascism is based on the idea of a cooperative state, Nazism is based on the Old Prussian idea of strong centralisation, imperialism and expansion. Their ideals are similar in that both Fascism and Nazism depend on chauvinism and are opposed to emigration of their peoples. Whereas in the Nazi party the element of anti-Semitism plays a prominent role, it is entirely lacking in Fascism.

'The substance of Fascism is Mussolini's personality; the same applies in a much lesser degree to Hitler. Mussolini has the intellect and bearing of a martial hero. Hitler has the intellect of a crusading sectarian leader, oblivious to dangers which surround him but with intense energy and being relentless in the pursuit of his aims.'

'So, Hitler feels as though he has the backing of crucial industrialists. But what about the bankers?'

'The Brüning Government, by emergency decrees, has established a situation which under certain circumstances would enable a complete transition to government by dictatorship without upsetting the country. Banking, commerce and industry are already accustomed to function under a semi-dictatorial government and the change to a Hitler dictatorship would not be great, provided Hitler did not impose compulsory measures.'

'What about the trade unions? Surely without their support he would have very little chance of achieving his ambitions.'

'Good question. It is doubtful Hitler would succeed in bringing the trade unions under a Nazi national dictatorship. The existing trade unions make up the Social-Democratic Party. They oppose a dictatorship and constitute the strongest opposition to Hitler, and the two movements are irreconcilable. The strongest of these are the trade unions controlled by the Social Democrats, which are in control of communications and the key industries. The conservative Catholic trade unions are next in strength. They constitute the Left wing of the Centre Party and are linked with the Social Democrats. The rest of the trade unions are under the control of the Communists. The workers controlled by Hitler are principally those who represent the floating labour sector, who lack the disciplined organisation of the trade unionists. They are also apt to drop away from Hitler the minute the depression ends. The trade unionists possess a most powerful weapon opposing Hitler – the general strike. The Nazis, on the other hand, claim that their SA troops are organised principally for the purpose of dealing with internal disorders and would be able to cope with a general strike ...'

'So it would seem Hitler has a battle in front of him to gain power?'

'It's not a *lay down misère* for him but he has plenty of other support. Hitler, particularly recently, has taken a very strong stand to obtain the

110

favour of international private banking groups. He has promised them full payment of Germany's private debts, but not 'a cent of tribute,' that is, the cancellation of all political debts, reparations, etc. His purpose was to reassure them and, quite obviously, to gain their support in opposing the French reparations demands.'

'So where do you think Germany now stands?'

'Hitler's patriotic utterances in general resemble those of Mussolini a few years ago – national war cries without defined objective. Both Hitler and Mussolini demand territorial expansion for their peoples. Hitler apparently hopes to achieve the union of all German nations, that is, Austria and Germany; and the return of all former German territory – Memel, Danzig, Upper Silesia, and Alsace-Lorraine – under a strongly federalised German state. He also demands the return of German colonies. Hitler's war cries, especially up to last December, greatly resembled those of Mussolini a few years ago. Now he is endeavouring to be more diplomatic, especially in order not to offend Great Britain, Italy and us.

'The policies of Hitler, especially in the field of foreign affairs and the economic reform of Germany are still unclear to us.'

'They don't seem too worried about upsetting the French.'

'No, you're right, following Hitler's recent interview with representatives of the American, French and British press in Berlin. The French press showed strong interest in the Nazis' aspirations. A spirit of dismay, uneasiness and alarm characterised the French editorial comment. The French Nationalist press seems to be in constant fear of a Nazi-led Germany, and also of an alliance between Hitler and Mussolini. The French Government points to the agitation of the Nazis as an argument in support of the French demands for security.'

'Thank you Bill, that was a very comprehensive and informative briefing. I think it is important to exchange notes, as it were. On a regular basis.'

'I agree.'

Jack left the 'Ambassador's office with a certain amount of trepidation.

# 26. The Rise and Rise of Hitler

## Berlin 1933

Jack, in his role as Military Attaché, had the opportunity of meeting Adolf Hitler in a private meeting in his office at the Reichstag.

It was only a five-minute meeting and not much of import was discussed, but Hitler did stress how highly he regarded the United States of America and how important the two countries' friendship was to Germany.

Jack watched, listened and reported back to Washington the events of what was a tumultuous year, not just for Germany but for the world.

## January 1933

Hitler became Chancellor of a coalition government, where the Nazis had a third of the seats in the Reichstag.

## February 1933

The German Reichstag was destroyed by fire. The plot and execution was almost certainly due to the Nazis but they point the finger at the Communists and trigger a General Election.

## March 1933

The Enabling Act passed – powers of legislation passed to Hitler's cabinet for four years, making him virtual dictator.

Hitler proclaimed the Nazi Party as the only political party permitted in Germany. All other parties and trade unions were disbanded. Individual German states lost their autonomous powers, while Nazi officials became state governors.

# April 1933

Communist Party was banned.

# May 1933

Socialists, Trade Unions and strikes are banned.

# October 1933

Hitler withdrew from the League of Nations. In the following months, he trebled the size of the German Army and ignored the arms restrictions imposed by the Treaty of Versailles.

# A year of change by any standards

# June 1934

# Night of the Long Knives

The Night of the Long Knives, in June 1934, saw the elimination of the Brown Shirts' or SA's leadership, and others who had angered Hitler in the recent past in Nazi Germany. After this date, the SS lead by Heinrich Himmler, became far more powerful in Nazi Germany.

For all the power the Enabling Act gave Hitler, he still felt threatened by some in the Nazi Party. He was also worried that the regular Army had not given an oath of allegiance. Hitler knew that the army hierarchy held him in disdain, as he was 'only' a corporal in their eyes. The Night of the Long Knives not only removed the SA leaders but also got Hitler the Army's oath that he so needed.

By the summer of 1934, the SA's numbers had swollen to two million men. They were under the control of Ernst Röhm, a loyal follower of Hitler since the early days of the Nazi Party. The SA had given the Nazis an iron fist with which to disrupt other political parties meetings before January 1933. The SA was also used to enforce law after Hitler became Chancellor in January 1933. To all intents, they were the enforcers of the Nazi Party and there is no evidence that Röhm was ever planning anything against Hitler.

However, Röhm had made enemies within the Nazi Party – Himmler, Goering and Goebbels were angered by the power he had gained and convinced Hitler that this was a threat to his position.

By June 1934, the regular Army hierarchy also saw the SA as a threat to their authority. The SA outnumbered the Army by 1934 and Röhm had openly spoken about taking over the regular Army by absorbing it into the SA. Such talk alarmed the Army's leaders.

By the summer of 1934, Hitler had decided that Röhm was a 'threat' and he made a pact with the Army. If Röhm and the other SA leaders were removed, the rank and file SA men would come under the control of the Army but the Army would have to swear an oath of loyalty to Hitler. The Army agreed and Röhm's fate was sealed.

On the nights of 29$^{th}$ and 30$^{th}$ June 1934, units of the SS arrested the leaders of the SA and other political opponents. Men such as Gregor Strasser, von Schleicher and von Bredow were arrested despite neither of them having any connection with Röhm. The arrests were carried on for two more nights.

Seventy-seven men were executed on charges of treason, although historians tend to think the figure is higher. The SA was brought to heel and placed under the command of the Army. Hitler received an oath of allegiance from all those who served in the Army. Röhm was shot. Others were bludgeoned to death.

The first the public officially knew about the event was on 13$^{th}$ July 1934, when Hitler told the Reichstag which now met in the Kroll Opera House, Berlin, that for the duration of the arrests he and he alone was the judge in Germany and that the SS carried out his orders. From that time on, the SS led by Heinrich Himmler became a feared force in Nazi Germany. The efficiency with which the SS had carried out its orders greatly impressed Hitler and Himmler was to acquire huge power base within Nazi Germany.

## July 1934

After the death of President Hindenburg, Hitler became *Führer and Reichskanzler* and abolished the title of President.

## 26<sup>th</sup> February 1935

Hitler ordered Hermann Goering to establish the Luftwaffe, the German air force, in defiance of the terms of the Treaty of Versailles.

## March 1935

Hitler publicly announced that the German Army was to be expanded. Conscription was introduced.

## 15<sup>th</sup> September 1935

Nuremberg Laws defined German citizenship. Relationships between Jews and Aryans were banned.

As each year passed during their stay in Germany more and more worrying events took place. Washington knew of each and every event; they didn't need Jack to report them yet they valued his opinions and interpretation of what was happening.

Jack and Anna tried to lead reasonably normal lives while Hitler's campaign of terror and intimidation was taking place in the streets of Berlin. Jack was called to assist a number of American citizens who were either bashed or imprisoned for not raising their arms and shouting '*Heil Hitler*' as they were required to do. 'Good evening' or 'good morning' was no longer acceptable.

They had met some nice German people during their stay and had been invited to dinner a number of times. It was at one such dinner party at a prominent industrialist's nineteenth century town house in the beautiful area of Charlottenburg that they understood how Hitler had changed Berliner's lives.

In previous gatherings the conversation was open and frank when it came to German politics. On this occasion none of the guests were willing to talk about, let alone discuss, Hitler or what was happening inside Germany.

When Jack and Anna departed, the host Karl Bauer escorted them to the street where the embassy car was waiting.

> 'I am sorry, but things now are so bad we do not dare mention anything about what is happening for fear we will be reported to the SS and who knows what!'

> 'Don't worry Karl, we understand the situation.'

# 27. Let the Games Begin

Soon after Hitler took power in 1933, observers in the United States and other western democracies questioned the morality of supporting an Olympic Games hosted by the Nazi regime. It had been awarded the games in 1931 prior to Hitler coming to power. Responding to reports of the persecution of Jewish athletes in 1933, Avery Brundage, president of the American Olympic Committee (AOC), stated:

> *The very foundation of the modern Olympic revival will be undermined if individual countries are allowed to restrict participation by reason of class, creed, or race.*

Brundage, like many others in the Olympic movement, initially considered moving the Games from Germany. After a brief and tightly managed inspection of German sports facilities in 1934, Brundage stated publicly that Jewish athletes were being treated fairly and that the Games should go on, as planned.

## England 1936

Julie and Harry had settled into their seventeenth-century manor house left to them by his mother and father. The Earl and Duchess had been killed in a motor vehicle accident while they were travelling from the family castle, Raby, to their Surrey manor house in 1934.

Harry and Julie were now the Earl and Duchess of Westmoreland and were now the custodians of Raby Castle and Westmoreland Manor.

**Westmoreland Manor**

Although they were titled, they tended to use their professional names, Dr Harold de Neville and Dr Julie Doherty.

They decided to attend the Berlin Games. It would give them the opportunity to see Julie's brother, Jack and soak in the atmosphere of the Games. They did have concerns about the Nazis but decided to put them aside for the sake of the visit.

Julie telephoned Jack.

'Hello Jack, it's Julie, how are you?'

'Julie! Hello! I'm good thanks. And you?

'We're both well.'

'I suppose I should be calling you Duchess from now on.' Jack couldn't resist a dig at her new status.

'Don't be silly Jack! Now listen, Harry and I have decided to come to the Olympic Games and wonder if you'd like a couple of visitors?'

'That would be great! I'm sure Anna will agree with me. We'd love to have you come and stay. How soon before the Games start will you be arriving?

'We thought we might get to Berlin on the 30th July – that would give us a couple of days before the opening ceremony on the 1st August.'

'I just need to get clearance from the Ambassador as our house in on Embassy grounds but I am sure there will be no problem. I'll send you a telegram confirming if that's OK.'

'Harry and I are really looking forward to seeing you both. Goodbye Jack.'

'Goodbye … Duchess!'

Harry and Julie flew to Berlin on Thursday 30<sup>th</sup> July and were met at the airport by Jack and Anna with an Embassy car. After the initial hugs and kisses they began their journey to the Embassy compound.

'They love their Nazi swastikas don't they Jack? They're on every bloody building,' commented Harry.

'They sure do Harry, they want to make sure everybody knows who's running the show.'

'Is it as bad as what we read back home, about the Jews?'

'I'm afraid so. Hitler ordered all the anti-Jew signs to be taken down for the duration of the Games but believe you me, they'll be up hours after the closing ceremony. They are being persecuted, as are the left-wingers; Communists and such. This is a draconian administration. You cannot talk like this – even as a foreigner – if there's a chance someone might hear you.'

'So how do you go about your business and your lives when all this is going on?'

'Very carefully.'

They pulled into the expansive US Embassy, and the Cadillac stopped outside a delightful bungalow with ivy growing up its white façade.

'Well, this is it. Home,' said Anna.

'It looks delightful Anna. I'm sure we will love our stay here,' said Julie as she opened the car door, eager to see inside.

It was in fact delightful. Their room looked out to a private courtyard with a rose garden in full bloom.

'This is just beautiful, you two, no wonder you have stayed so long.'

'Sis, the reason we have stayed so long is I've been ordered to stay here. We don't really have a choice. However, living here makes it tolerable.'

119

The driver grabbed their luggage while Harry and Julie were given a tour of the house.

'Thank you, Anna and Jack. For putting us up. As it were.'

'Our pleasure. Now, Ambassador Dodd has invited us all for dinner tonight. Just casual. No need for a tuxedo, Harry.'

'Well, that's good considering I didn't pack one. I do have a lounge suit – would that be suitable?'

'That'll be fine.'

'I take it you have packed some nice frocks Julie?'

'Yes Jack, you know me well.' She laughed.

'OK, we'll leave you to unpack. Let's say 6.30 pm in the lounge for a pre-dinner drink and then over to the Embassy for 7.30 pm dinner.'

'Sounds good.'

Over dinner, in the sanctuary of the US Embassy and in the company of the Ambassador William Dodd and his delightful wife Mattie, they had a very frank discussion

'So, Mr Ambassador have you met Hitler yet?' asked Julie naïvely.

'Please call me Bill. Yes Julie. I had to wait about two months to see the German Führer. Normally an Ambassador from a major power such as ours would wait two weeks after taking up the post.'

'What was he like, Bill? Intimidating? Or comical?'

'Certainly not comical. I arrived at Bismarck's former palace where Hitler has his quarters. It was quite daunting, climbing up a very wide set of marble stairs guarded at every landing and turn by a Nazi SS soldier with their hands raised in Roman style.'

'Did you feel compelled to return the Hitler salute, Bill?' asked Harry.

'I just bowed my head slightly. I certainly wasn't going to comply with their ridiculous laws regarding salutations. I waited in his ante-room until the Minister for Foreign Affairs von Neurath invited me into the Chancellor's office, a room some fifty feet square with tables and chairs scattered about for group conferences.'

'Did you feel nervous at all?' Jack inquired.

'No Jack, not really. I certainly sat there in great anticipation, not knowing really what to expect.'

'Did he goose-step in wearing his elaborate uniform?' Anna asked, with an impish look on her face.

'Anna! Of course not, in fact I was quite surprised he had dressed in a simple lounge suit, neat and erect-looking. Better in person than he had appeared in newspaper photos I had seen.'

'Bill, are you permitted to divulge what you discussed with him?' asked Jack.

'It wasn't all confidential Jack. I raised the assaults upon Americans and the discriminations against American creditors. He seemed very concerned. The German dictator even assured me that future attacks against US citizens in Nazi Germany would be strictly punished and that he would issue decrees that foreigners were not obliged to offer the Nazi salute.'

'So you had a win on your first meeting with 'the great Man'!'

'Hmm, not entirely. The conversation turned to Nazi Germany's withdrawal the previous Saturday from the League of Nations. I called it a 'thunderbolt', totally unexpected. This really started him off. He ranted about the Treaty of Versailles, the failure of the powers to keep their promises about disarmament and the indignity of keeping Germany in a defenceless status.

'We discussed various other matters, which I am not at liberty to divulge. I departed after about forty-five minutes.'

'What was your overall impression of Hitler, Bill?'

Probably the Führer's belligerence and self-confidence. He's certainly a man not to be taken lightly.'

'Well I'm sure it is a meeting you will never forget,' said Harry.

William Dodd's final assessment of Hitler and his regime was as follows:

'The Hitler regime is composed of ... rather inexperienced and very dogmatic persons, all of whom have been more or less connected with murderous undertakings in the last eight or ten years. It is a combination of men who represent different groups of the present German majority, not an actual majority.'

By this point of his stay in Nazi Germany, the US ambassador had lost a bit of his naïveté. Concerning Hitler, Dodd wrote,

He has definitely said on a number of occasions that a people survives by fighting and dies as a consequence of peaceful policies. His influence is, and has been, wholly belligerent ... In the back of his mind is the old German idea of dominating Europe through warfare.

Dodd's final realisation of the threat posed by Hitler came too late, as by then he was unable to effectively use his post to urge Washington, London and Paris to oppose Hitler's consolidation of control over Germany.

# 1ˢᵗ August 1936

## Olympic Games

Jack had organised excellent seats for the party of four through his connections at the Embassy.

They arrived at the Olympic stadium two hours before the official start. The detailed program they received at the Embassy looked amazing.

*Parade of dignitaries to either Mass (St. Hedwig's) or a Protestant service (Evangelical Cathedral)*

*Olympic Flame Welcoming Ceremony at the Lustgarten with Hitler Youth*

*Parade of dignitaries to the Olympic Stadium*

*Hindenburg Airship flies over the stadium with 'XI. Olympiade Berlin 1936' painted on its side*

*Hitler arrives at the May Field (staging area next to the Olympic Stadium) - Olympic Fanfare by Paul Winter performed from Marathon Towers of the stadium by military band*

*Hitler enters the stadium to 'March of Homage' by Wagner - Hitler is greeted by small girl who salutes him with 'Heil, mein Führer' and presents him with flowers as an Introductory Theme by Herbert Windt is performed*

*German National Anthem performed while every participating country's flag is raised on poles surrounding the top of the stadium*

*Olympic Bell rung - inscribed across it 'I summon the youth of the world'*

*Parade of Nations*

*Recording of Baron Pierre de Coubertain's voice played - the same quote used in the 1932 Olympics*

*Hitler declares the games open*

*Olympic Flag raised - simultaneously: artillery guns fire, 20,000 carrier pigeons released, fanfare played from the Marathon Towers, mass orchestra and choir perform the Olympic Hymn conducted and written by Richard Strauss*

*Olympic Cauldron lit by Fritz Schilgen - German 1500 meter athlete who failed to make the German team, selected for his beautiful and graceful running style*

*Athlete's Oath*

*Handel's Hallelujah Chorus performed by 3,000 singers and orchestra*

*Athletes parade out of the stadium followed by Concluding Fanfare by Paul Winter*

*OLYMPIC YOUTH – mass play by Carl Diem – music by Carl Orff (performed under the floodlight at night)*

*Part 1: Children at Play – 2,500 girls 11-12 and 900 boys run into the stadium for the grand stairs and tunnel; dance; form the Olympic Rings; leave Part 2: Maidenly Grace – 2,300 girls 14-18 flood into the stadium; one begins a waltz; games follow with balls, hoops, and clubs; large group dance; form circle at one end of the stadium*

*Part 3: Youth at Play in a Serious Mood – thousands of boys flood field; sing and divide up into different national 'campfires'; fight each other; thousands of flags of all the nations enter and march around the track while boys salute; forest of flags surround the cauldron while child recites poem 'Hymn of Fire'*

*Part 4: Heroic Struggle and Death Lament – along the track advance dancing warriors each with a leader; leaders duel in a dance, one falls, the other wounded also falls; leaders led off the field in death procession; mass dance 'lamentation' performed by all; Beethoven's Ninth, Fourth Mvt.*

123

*begins; floodlights form dome of light over stadium; thousands of torches and flags wave on the track during the Ode to Joy.*

No other Olympic Games had such an impressive opening ceremony. This was the first Olympics to use the 'eternal flame' with runners starting at Mount Olympus and finishing in Berlin ten days later.

The group were close to the 'Mayfield', a grass area where the equestrian events took place; close to where Hitler and his cronies would be seated. When Hitler entered the arena the German crowd stood with their right arms outstretched yelling '*Heil Hitler*'. The intensity and excitement in the arena almost persuaded Jack and Anna, and Harry and Julie to follow suit. They could now understand how he motivated the German people and terrorised the Jews.

When the German Olympic team entered the arena the largely German crowd again rose with the Nazi salute.

When back in the quiet sanctuary of the American Embassy they poured themselves a drink and reflected on what was a spectacular, yet frightening, experience.

They all looked forward to the first day of competition the next day. They would be returning to the Olympic stadium for track and field. The three Americans in the group were looking forward to seeing the young Jesse Owens run and jump over the next few days.

Arriving at the stadium early, they took their seats ready to cheer on their heroes.

The first gold Jesse won was in the 100 metres, where Owens edged out teammate Ralph Metcalfe in a time of 10.3 seconds.

Gold number two came the next day in the long jump, where he fouled on his first two attempts. One was just a practice run where he continued down the runway into the pit, but German officials didn't buy it and counted it as a jump. Top German long-jumper Luz Long suggested Owens play it safe and jump a few inches before the usual take-off spot. He took his advice and qualified for the finals, where he won the gold with a leap of 26 feet 5½ inches. Long was there to congratulate him.

'It took a lot of courage for him to befriend me in front of Hitler,' Owens would later say. 'You can melt down all the medals and cups I have and they wouldn't be a plating on the 24-karat friendship I felt for Luz Long at that moment.'

The third gold was in the 200-metre dash, where he defeated, among others, Jackie Robinson's older brother Mack, and broke the Olympic record with a time of 20.7 seconds.

Gold number four was a controversial one – not with the Germans, but with his fellow Americans. American Jews Marty Glickman and Sam Stoller were supposed to run for the United States on the 4x100 relay team. At the last minute, Owens and Metcalfe replaced them and it was reported that Hitler asked US officials not to embarrass him any further by having two Jews win gold in Berlin. Whether that's true or not, the Owens-led US team rolled to victory in a world record time of 39.8 seconds and Owens' magical Olympics came to a close.

While German officials denounced Owens, an overwhelming majority of the German fans treated him like a hero. In 1984, a street in Berlin was named in his honour.

Everyone knows that at the 1936 Olympics Hitler snubbed Jesse Owens. As the story goes, after Owens won one gold medal, Hitler, incensed, stormed out of Olympic Stadium so he wouldn't have to congratulate Owens on his victory.

Such a performance would have been perfectly in character, but it didn't happen. William J. Baker, Owens's biographer, says the newspapers made up the whole story. Owens himself originally insisted it wasn't true, but eventually he began saying it was, apparently out of sheer boredom with the issue.

The truth of the matter was Hitler did not congratulate Owens, but that day he didn't congratulate anybody else either, not even the German winners. As a matter of fact, Hitler didn't congratulate anyone after the first day of the competition. That first day he had shaken hands with all the German victors, but that got him in trouble with the members of the Olympic Committee. They told him that to maintain Olympic neutrality, he would have to congratulate everyone, or no one. Hitler chose to honour no one.

Harry and Julie also attended the swimming and the rowing then returned to England before the closing ceremony.

The results of the 1936 Berlin Olympic Games

| Country | G | S | B | TOT |
| --- | --- | --- | --- | --- |
| Germany | 38 | 31 | 32 | 101 |
| USA | 24 | 21 | 12 | 57 |
| Italy | 9 | 13 | 5 | 27 |
| Sweden | 5 | 10 | 21 | 36 |
| Finland | 6 | 6 | 20 | 32 |
| Japan | 6 | 4 | 10 | 20 |
| France | 7 | 6 | 6 | 19 |
| Switz | 4 | 9 | 5 | 18 |
| Austria | 5 | 7 | 5 | 17 |
| Neth | 6 | 4 | 7 | 17 |
| Hungary | 10 | 1 | 5 | 16 |
| UK | 4 | 7 | 3 | 14 |
| Canada | 1 | 3 | 5 | 9 |
| Czech | 3 | 5 | 1 | 9 |
| Poland | 0 | 4 | 5 | 9 |
| Argentina | 2 | 2 | 3 | 7 |
| Estonia | 2 | 2 | 3 | 7 |
| Norway | 3 | 2 | 6 | 11 |
| Denmark | 0 | 2 | 3 | 5 |
| Egypt | 2 | 1 | 2 | 5 |
| Belgium | 0 | 0 | 3 | 3 |
| Mexico | 0 | 3 | 3 | 6 |
| Latvia | 0 | 1 | 1 | 2 |
| Turkey | 1 | 0 | 1 | 2 |
| Australia | 0 | 0 | 1 | 1 |
| India | 1 | 0 | 0 | 1 |
| NZ | 1 | 0 | 0 | 1 |
| Phili | 0 | 0 | 1 | 1 |
| Portugal | 0 | 0 | 1 | 1 |
| Romania | 0 | 1 | 0 | 1 |
| SA | 0 | 1 | 0 | 1 |
| Yugos | 1 | 0 | 1 | 2 |

Hitler got his wish: Germany dominated the medal count proving to the world Germany was a superior nation; an enormous propaganda win for the Nazis.

# 28.Hitler's March to War

Jack sent monthly reports back to Washington, each one more ominous than the previous. It was becoming obvious that Hitler was preparing Germany for war.

## 25th October 1936

Axis alliance concluded between Germany and Italy.

## 25th November 1936

Anti-Comintern pact concluded between Germany and Japan.

Joachim von Ribbentrop negotiated an agreement between Germany and Japan that declared the hostility of the two countries to international communism. In case of an unprovoked attack by the Soviet Union against Germany or Japan, the two nations agreed to consult on what measures to take 'to safeguard their common interests'. They also agreed that neither nation would make any political treaties with the Soviet Union. Germany also agreed to recognise the Japanese puppet regime in Manchuria.

## December 1936

Law concerning the Hitler Youth made membership of the Hitler Youth compulsory for all boys.

## 14th March 1938

*Anschluss* (union) with Austria, annexing the smaller nation into a greater Germany. Hitler made a triumphant entry into Vienna.

## 30th September 1938

The Munich Agreement was a settlement permitting Nazi Germany's annexation of Czechoslovakia's areas along the country's borders mainly inhabited by

German speakers, for which a new territorial designation 'Sudetenland' was coined. The agreement was negotiated at a conference held in Munich, Germany, among the major powers of Europe without the presence of Czechoslovakia.

## November 1938

*Kristallnacht* (Night of Crystal). The sounds of breaking glass shattered the air in cities throughout Germany while fires across the country devoured synagogues and Jewish institutions. By the end of the rampage, gangs of Nazi stormtroopers had destroyed seven thousand Jewish businesses, set fire to more than nine hundred synagogues, killed ninety-one Jews and deported some thirty thousand Jewish men to concentration camps.

## 15$^{th}$ March 1939

Hitler invaded and occupied Czechoslovakia in contravention of the Munich Agreement. The Nazi war machine now controlled 66 percent of Czechoslovakia's coal, 70 percent of its iron and steel, and 70 percent of its electrical power. Without those resources, the Czech nation was left vulnerable to complete German domination.

## 31$^{st}$ March 1939

Britain issued a statement guaranteeing Poland's independence. The issuing of this statement meant that if Germany invaded Poland, Britain would come to the aid of the Poles.

## 15$^{th}$ April 1939

Jack received orders to leave the American Embassy in Berlin and transfer to the Embassy in London. He did not need to be persuaded, things were getting well and truly out of hand in Germany.

He was allocated a two-bedroom suite at The Savoy Hotel and an office in the US Headquarters in Grosvenor House.

## Berlin September 1939

The Germans concocted a story of Polish troops crossing their border and firing on various installations. In supposed retaliation, German tanks rolled across the Polish border during the early hours of September 1st, 1939. Tensions were running high throughout Europe. Britain and France began mobilisation of their armies while Italy's Mussolini desperately tried to convince Hitler to forestall war. The British and French representatives met with German Foreign Minister Ribbentrop warning that they would fulfil their obligation to Poland and go to war if German forces did not withdraw from Polish territory.

Paul Schmidt was a translator in the German Foreign Ministry and present at the history-making events of those last days of peace in Europe.

It is just after midnight on 3rd September 1939 and the German juggernaut continues to slam its way into Poland. The Germans had not responded to an earlier British and French demand to withdraw their troops and a message is received stating that Sir Neville Henderson, the British Ambassador to Germany, wishes to meet with German Foreign Minister Ribbentrop. It is obvious to all that the Ambassador's message will probably mean war. Ribbentrop decides that the translator Schmidt should meet with the British ambassador alone: he was a bit busy.

It was after midnight when the British Embassy telephoned Schmidt to say that Henderson had received instructions from London to transmit a communication from his Government at 9 am and that he asked to be received by Ribbentrop at the Foreign Office at that time. It was clear that this communication could contain nothing agreeable, and that it might possibly be a real ultimatum. Ribbentrop in consequence showed not the slightest inclination to receive the British Ambassador personally next morning.

> 'Schmidt, you should receive the Ambassador in my place. Just ask the English whether that will suit them, and say that the Foreign Minister is not available at 9 o'clock.'

> 'The English agreed, and therefore I was instructed to receive Henderson next morning – that is, in five hours time, it being now 4 o'clock in the morning.'

> Schmidt described the meeting:

> 'On Sunday, 3rd September 1939, after the pressure of work over the last few days, I overslept, and had to take a taxi to the Foreign Office. I could just see Henderson entering the building as I drove across the Wilhelmsplatz. I used a side entrance and stood in Ribbentrop's office ready to receive Henderson punctually at 9 o'clock. Henderson was

announced as the hour struck. He came in looking very serious, shook hands, but declined my invitation to be seated, remaining standing in the middle of the room. "I regret that on the instructions of my Government I have to hand you an ultimatum for the German Government," he said with deep emotion and then, with both of us still standing, he read out the British ultimatum.

More than twenty-four hours have elapsed since an immediate reply was requested to the warning of 1st September and since then the attacks on Poland have been intensified. If His Majesty's Government has not received satisfactory assurances of the cessation of all aggressive action against Poland, and the withdrawal of German troops from that country by 11 o'clock British Summer Time, from that time a state of war will exist between Great Britain and Germany.

'When he had finished reading, Henderson handed me the ultimatum and bade me goodbye, saying: "I am sincerely sorry that I must hand such a document to you in particular, as you have always been most anxious to help."

'I too expressed my regret, and added a few heartfelt words. I always had the highest regard for the British Ambassador.

**Ambassador Henderson Leaving the German Foreign Office**

'I then took the ultimatum to the Chancellery, where everyone was anxiously awaiting me. Most of the members of the Cabinet and the leading men of the Party were collected in the room next to Hitler's office. There was something of a crush and I had difficulty in getting through to Hitler.

### Hitler Seated at His Desk

'When I entered the next room Hitler was sitting at his desk and Ribbentrop stood by the window. Both looked up expectantly as I came in. I stopped at some distance from Hitler's desk, and then slowly translated the British Government's ultimatum. When I finished, there was complete silence.

'Hitler sat immobile, gazing before him. He was not at a loss, as was afterwards stated, nor did he rage as others allege. He sat completely silent and unmoving.

'After an interval, which seemed an age, he turned to Ribbentrop, who had remained standing by the window. "What now?" asked Hitler with a savage look, as though implying that his Foreign Minister had misled him about England's probable reaction? Ribbentrop answered quietly: "I assume that the French will hand in a similar ultimatum within the hour."

'As my duty was now performed, I withdrew. To those in the anteroom pressing round me I said: "The English have just handed us an ultimatum. In two hours a state of war will exist between England and Germany."

'In the anteroom, too, this news was followed by complete silence. Goering turned to me and said: "If we lose this war, then God have mercy on us!" Goebbels stood in a corner, downcast and self-absorbed. Everywhere in the room I saw looks of grave concern, even amongst the lesser Party people.'

# 29. WAR

## Again

### 3rd September 1939

Britain and France declared war on Germany on the morning of the 3rd September 1939.

That afternoon a U-boat captained by Fritz Julius Kemp fired on a passenger ship, the *Athenia* in the north-western sector of the Irish Sea. Despite the joint declaration of war, Hitler was still hopeful of a diplomatic resolution. He believed that he might yet be able to dissuade the Western Powers from war and to this end he issued strict orders for U-boats to follow the Prize Regulations. Under these regulations, attacks against passenger liners were prohibited, but unfortunately, the first ship that was sunk by a U-boat turned out to be a passenger liner. It caused an immediate furore in both Allied and neutral circles. It appeared that Germany was in favour of conducting unrestricted submarine warfare, as it had done during the First World War, which came so close to strangling the shipping lanes of Great Britain.

**The *Athenia***

This attack signalled the first casualties of a war that would cause over eighty million deaths including forty million civilians.

Not much happened after the sinking of the *Athenia*. This period was dubbed the 'Phoney War' and refers to what happened in Western Europe between September 1939 and the spring of 1940. To assume that nothing was going on in Europe would be wrong, as Poland was in the process of being occupied, with all that brought for the Polish people. However, in Western Europe very little of military importance did take place. In fact, so little occurred that many of the children who had been evacuated at the start of the war, had returned to their families. Neville Chamberlain had declared war, but nothing seemed to be actually happening.

During the Phoney War, Britain was also engaged in 'bombing' raids over Germany – but it was not bombs that were dropped, but propaganda leaflets. Sir Kingsley Wood, Secretary of State for War, called them 'truth raids'. The 'raids' served two purposes:

> The Germans would read about the evils of Nazi Germany.

> It would show the leaders of Germany just how vulnerable their country was to bombing raids.

Millions of leaflets were dropped over Germany. On 3$^{rd}$ September alone, 6 million copies of 'Note to the German People' were dropped in just one night – the equivalent of thirteen tons of paper. The main result of these initial raids was that the Germans stepped up their anti-aircraft batteries. While some politicians believed that the raids served a purpose, others in the military did not.

The English translation of the leaflet was:

# Warning: A Message from Great Britain

> *German Men and Women: 'The Government of the Reich have, with cold deliberation, forced war upon Great Britain. They have done so knowing that it must involve mankind in a calamity worse than that of 1914. The assurances of peaceful intentions the Fuehrer gave to you and to the world in April have proved as worthless as his words at the*

*Sportpalast last September, when he said: 'We have no more territorial claims to make in Europe'.*

*'Never has government ordered subjects to their death with less excuse. This war is utterly unnecessary. Germany was in no way threatened or deprived of justice.*

## Iron censorship

*Was she not allowed to re-enter the Rhineland, to achieve the* Anschluss, *and to take back the Sudeten Germans in peace? Neither we nor any other nation would have sought to limit her advance so long as she did not violate independent non-German peoples.*

*Every German ambition – just to others – might have been satisfied through friendly negotiation.'*

*President Roosevelt offered you both peace with honour and the prospect of prosperity. Instead, your rulers have condemned you to the massacre, miseries and privations of a war they cannot ever hope to win.*

*It is not us, but you they have deceived. For years their iron censorship has kept from you truths that even uncivilised peoples know.*

## Minds imprisoned

*It has imprisoned your minds in, as it were, a concentration camp. Otherwise they would not have dared to misrepresent the combination of peaceful peoples to secure peace as hostile encirclement.*

*We had no enmity against you, the German people.*

*This censorship has also concealed from you that you have not the means to sustain protracted warfare. Despite crushing taxation, you are on the verge of bankruptcy.*

*Our resources and those of our Allies, in men, arms and supplies are immense. We are too strong to break by blows and we could wear you down inexorably.*

*You, the German people, can, if you will, insist on peace at any time. We also desire peace, and are prepared to conclude it with any peace loving Government in Germany.*

# 30. Military Intelligence

## Is a Contradiction in Terms.

### *Groucho Marx*

Jack had been sending reports to the Under Secretary of the Navy, Eugene Leutze, about his view of the war in Europe. Poland had been completely vanquished in just over a month. He reported that France was under real threat as well as Finland and Norway. His predictions proved correct.

Two days after Britain and France declared war on Germany the United States declared their neutrality.

That was not to say that America did not take a keen interest in the European conflict. She knew that whatever happened in Europe would have a major effect on the American economy. The Jewish lobby also was putting a great deal of pressure on Roosevelt and his administration.

Jack worked closely with MI6, the British secret service. America did not have a consolidated intelligence service, consequently each arm of the military were responsible for their own intelligence. Replication of information was prolific.

The first half of 1940 proved very successful for the Germans and disastrous for the Allies.

9$^{th}$ April 1940 Nazis invade Denmark and Norway.

10$^{th}$ May 1940 Nazis invade France, Belgium, Luxembourg and the Netherlands.

15$^{th}$ May 1940 Holland surrenders to the Nazis.

Jack reported back to Washington.

June 19, 1940

Dear Sir,

As you are already aware, Nazi Germany has been successful in invading France, Belgium, Luxembourg and the Netherlands in the last month. These gains on top of their previous conquests have given Nazi Germany control of vast natural resources to support their war effort. The British have a real fear that Hitler will mount an invasion in the next few months.

Britain and France have been our friends for many years and I do not think a German invasion would be in our best interests.

The Nazi war machine would be stopped in their tracks if it weren't for the unrivalled production of trucks and other motor vehicles to transport troops and supplies.

American corporations, mainly Ford and General Motors, are producing those trucks and motor vehicles.

I am aware that Jim Mooney President of General Motors Overseas is on very friendly terms with Hitler who he as met several times.

I enclose a brief biography of Mooney and his activities of late.

Biography

James D. Mooney is a qualified engineer and corporate executive. He was born in Cleveland, Ohio on 18 February 1884. In 1908, he received a Bachelor of Science from the Case School of Applied Sciences in Mining and Metallurgy. Mooney left soon after graduation for gold mining expeditions in Mexico and California. Between 1910 and 1917, he worked successively at Westinghouse, B. F. Goodrich and Hyatt Roller Bearing Company during which time he became increasingly involved in corporate management. In 1917, at the age of thirty-three, he enlisted and served as a captain in France with the 309th Ammunition Regiment, 159th Field Artillery. At the close of the war, Mooney was named President and General Manager of the Remy Electric Company, a subsidiary of General Motors Corporation. In 1922, he became a Vice-President of GMC and President of General Motors Overseas, a company that trades in over one hundred countries. As part of his responsibilities in managing overseas production, Mooney has travelled extensively throughout the world, visiting GMC's numerous manufacturing and assembly plants. In this capacity, he has been afforded the opportunity to meet with senior government officials and others in positions of power and influence.

My concern with Mooney relates to his quasi-official involvement in international affairs. He has been acting largely on his own volition, although it would seem with official sanction.

He believes he can apply methods of corporate negotiation to international moderation. He sees himself as a modern diplomat with his methods being used as the standard for all future diplomacy. Mooney has expressed the inadequacies of traditional diplomacy by arguing that diplomats are frequently 'willing to risk millions of lives rather than to try to see the other side and to arrive at conclusions which involve some give-and-take on both sides, but which are cheaper than the resort to war.'

I have been able to determine whom Mooney met with while visiting Germany and England.

1. May 1939: Joe Kennedy and Helmuth Wohlthat meet in the spring of 1939. Mooney was called to Germany to discuss a number of issues with the Nazi government pertaining to GMC's Adam-Opel plant. In the process, he became aware of interest in securing gold loans in exchange for an agreement to stop Germany's practice of subsidised exports and special exchange practices. It was Mooney who arranged a meeting between Ambassador Joseph Kennedy and Helmuth Wohlthat, a member of Goering's staff working on Germany's 'Four Year Plan.' The Meeting was held in London on May 9, 1939.

2. December 1939 and January 1940: Roosevelt-Mooney meetings.

Mooney has become convinced that hostilities in Europe could be subsided through the intercession of neutral third party moderation. It is my understanding that Mooney presented his views to President Roosevelt at two meetings, on December 22, 1939 and January 24, 1940. It is believed that President Roosevelt agreed to use Mooney's influence to initiate 'discussion' on an informal basis.

3. March 1940: Hitler, Goering and Mooney meetings.

We know Mooney met with Hitler on March 4, 1939 and with Goering on March 7. The Hitler-Mooney meeting included Mooney's presentation of Presidents Roosevelt's 'informal and unofficial attitudes'.

Hitler replied citing the 'unfortunate rumours' distorting German and American relations; the extent of Germany's war aims; the unity of the German people behind the Reich; and the economic security of Germany, among other topics.

The Goering-Mooney meeting included a presentation of President Roosevelt's views, a discussion of German and American relations, American public opinion regarding Finland and various economic issues, concentrating on most-favoured-nation practices.

I am sure you are aware Mooney received the German Eagle with Cross, the highest medal Hitler awarded to foreign commercial collaborators and supporters.

Mooney, albeit a staunch supporter of Hitler and his Nazi regime, is not the driving force behind General Motors' commitment to produce motor vehicles for Germany's war machine. It is Alfred P. Sloan President of General Motors headquartered in Detroit. His firm belief is that General Motors could and should create its own foreign policy, and back the Hitler regime even as we recoil from it.

'Industry must assume the role of enlightened industrial statesmanship,' Sloan declared in an April 1936 quarterly report to GM stockholders. 'It can no longer confine its responsibilities to the mere physical production and distribution of goods and services. It must aggressively move forward and attune its thinking and its policies toward advancing the interest of the community at large, from which it receives a most valuable franchise.'

In ramping up auto production in the Nazi Reich, Sloan understands that he is not just manufacturing vehicles. Sloan and Hitler both know that GM, by creating wealth and shrinking unemployment, is helping to prop up the Hitler regime.

I am also concerned that powerful business people such as Mooney, Sloan and Ford are providing information and recommendations to our President.

I will be dispatching further reports on Ford and others who have very close ties to the Nazis in a few days.

Sincerely

J Doherty

Brigadier General

# 31. You Can Have Any Colour As Long As It Is Black

Henry Ford

The Same Colour as the Nazi SS Uniform

## Henry Ford's Early Life

Henry Ford was born on 30th July 1863, on his family's farm in Wayne County, near Dearborn, Michigan. When Ford was fifteen years old, his father gave him a pocket watch, which the young boy promptly took apart and reassembled. Friends and neighbours were impressed, and requested that he fix their timepieces too. He obviously had a talent for all things mechanical.

Ford left home in 1878; he was not satisfied with farm work. He was now sixteen and was able to take up an apprenticeship as a machinist in Detroit. In the years that followed, he would learn to skilfully operate and service steam engines, and would also study bookkeeping.

## Early Career

In 1888, Ford married Clara Ala Bryant and briefly returned to farming to support his wife and son, Edsel. Three years later, he accepted a position as an engineer for the Edison Illuminating Company. In 1883, his natural talents earned him a promotion to Chief Engineer.

In his spare time Ford developed plans for a horseless carriage and in 1896, he constructed his first model called the 'Ford Quadricycle'. In the same year he attended a meeting with Edison executives and presented his automobile plans to Thomas Edison, who encouraged Ford to build a second and improved model.

## Ford Motor Company

In 1903 Ford established the Ford Motor Company. He introduced the Model T in October 1908. It was a great success, and the company grew by one hundred percent each year for its first ten years.

Ford became renowned for his revolutionary vision: the manufacture of an inexpensive automobile made by skilled workers earning good steady wages.

In 1914, he developed the first production line enabling mass production of Ford motorcars. His other great success was introducing the five-dollar per-day wage as a method of keeping the best workers loyal to his company.

Simple to drive and cheap to repair, half of all cars in America in 1918 were Model Ts.

## Ford the Anti-Semite

From a social perspective Henry Ford was marked by seemingly contradictory viewpoints. In business he offered profit sharing to select employees who stayed with the company for six months and conducted their lives in a respectable manner. The company's Social Department examined an employee's drinking and gambling habits to determine eligibility for participation.

Ford was opposed to World War I and fought hard for America to stay neutral. He funded a 'peace ship' to Europe.

In 1936, Ford and his family established the Ford Foundation to provide ongoing grants for research, education and development.

Yet Henry Ford was a committed anti-Semite.

His anti-Semitic views echoed the fears and assumptions of many Americans in the late 19th and 20th centuries. Anti-Semitism in America saw a change in expression and virulence when increased immigration from Europe brought millions of Jews to the US during Ford's childhood in the latter half of the nineteenth century. It reached its peak during the mid-nineteen twenties, a time when Ku Klux Klan membership had reached four million, prohibition laws had been enacted and discriminatory immigration policies had been passed favouring immigrants from northern and western Europe over other parts of the world.

A close friend of Henry's recalled a camping trip in 1919 during which Ford lectured a group around the campfire.

> 'He attributed all evil in the world to Jews – particularly the Jewish capitalists,' the friend wrote in his diary.

> 'The Jews caused the Great War, the Jews caused the outbreak of thieving and robbery all over the country, and the Jews caused the inefficiency of the navy...'

In 1918, Ford purchased his hometown newspaper, *The Dearborn Independent*. A year and a half later he began publishing a series of articles claiming a vast Jewish conspiracy was infecting America. The series ran in the following ninety-one issues. Ford had the articles bound into four volumes titled *The International Jew*. He organised to distribute half a million copies to his vast network of dealerships and subscribers. The rhetoric was not unusual in its content, but was in its scope. As one of the most famous and revered men in America, Henry Ford legitimised ideas that otherwise may have been given little credibility.

Henry became a close associate of Adolf Hitler and the senior people in his administration.

Ford Motors continued to build its close ties with Nazi Germany. Ford-Werke, the German subsidiary of Ford Motor Company, provided Hitler with a birthday gift of thirty five thousand Reichsmarks in April 1939. A letter from Ford-Werke read.

> The management of the Ford-Werke salutes our Führer with grateful heart, honesty, and allegiance, and, as before, pledges to cooperate in his life's work: achieving honour, liberty, and happiness for greater Germany and, indeed, for all peoples of Europe.

In 1940, Heinrich Albert, the director of Ford-Werke in Cologne, wrote back to the Michigan plant.

> *The 'Dementi' of Mr Henry Ford concerning war orders for Great Britain has greatly helped us.*

In October 1940 Edsel Ford, Henry's son, commended Ford-Werke for its operations in Germany.

Henry Ford's reward from Hitler came in July 1938, when on Ford's 75th birthday he was awarded the 'Grand Cross of the Supreme Order of the German Eagle'. This decoration was only the fourth ever given out by the Nazi Party. Benito Mussolini had been decorated with a similar honour earlier that same year. The German consul of Cleveland, Karl Kapp, and the German consul Fritz Hailer of Detroit made the presentation. The other American businessmen who received the honour were James Mooney from General Motors and Thomas Watson from IBM.

Other American supporters of Hitler and his Nazi regime were:

# Chase Manhattan Bank

The French branch froze Jewish accounts at the request of German occupation authorities during the war. Chase Manhattan's Paris branch manager, Carlos Niedermann, worked closely with German officials and approved loans to finance war production for the Nazi Army.

# IBM

The IBM-Nazi connection dated back to 1933 and continued throughout. IBM provided Hitler with billions of punch cards per year for the technology required to accelerate and automate all phases of its Jewish persecution and ultimately the holocaust.

# Bertelsmann Corporation

An American corporation, Bertelsmann cooperated with Hitler and the Nazi regime.

The company is presently the world's third largest publisher of English-language trade books with annual revenues of fourteen billion dollars

The company owns book clubs, magazines, newspapers, and music labels such as RCA. In the United States its holdings include Random House and Bantam Doubleday Dell publishing group, and it is a partner with Barnes & Noble.

Bertelsmann began to publish books during the early Hitler period that were used by Nazi propagandists. According to *The Nation*, the company issued a book geared for Nazis: *Dr Martin Luther's Little Catechism for the Man in*

146

*Brown* (*Der kleine Katechismus Dr Martin Luthers für den braunen Mann*), which praised Hitler and the Nazi movement and was also published by the company. In 1936 Bertelsmann brought out a popular edition of *People Without Space* (*Volk ohne Raum*) by Hans Grimm, an ardent Nazi supporter. The book was used to justify Hitler's expansionist attacks on Germany's neighbours. Throughout the thirties, Bertelsmann published bestsellers by authors favoured by Göbbels's propaganda ministry.

Jack reported back to Washington that along with GMC, Ford, IBM and Chase Manhattan Bank, other American companies were in close business relationships with the Nazis.

They included:

# Kodak

Kodak's German branch used slave labourers from concentration camps. Several of their other European branches did significant business with the Nazi government.

Wilhelm Keppler, one of Hitler's top economic advisers, had deep ties with Kodak. When Nazism began, Keppler advised Kodak and several other US companies that they'd benefit by firing all of their Jewish employees if they wished to conduct business with Nazi Germany.

# Hugo Boss

In the 1930s, Hugo Boss started making Nazi uniforms. Hugo Boss had joined the Nazi party, and got a contract to make the Hitler Youth, stormtrooper and SS uniforms.

This contract was very significant for Hugo Boss. The Nazis ensured Hugo became a prominent clothing manufacturer worldwide. The Nazi uniform contract went so well that Hugo Boss ended up needing to bring in slave labourers from Poland and France.

# Bayer

During the Holocaust, a German company, IG Farben manufactured the Zyklon-B gas used in the Nazi gas chambers. They also funded and helped with Josef Mengele's 'experiments' on concentration camp prisoners.

This company profited most from working with the Nazis. It was renamed Bayer after the war.

# 32.By the King's Command

## London, October 1940

Anna went to the front desk of the Savoy to collect the mail. She returned to their apartment, sat down in the living room and began sorting through the letters and bills. One letter caught her attention: it had the Royal Coat of Arms on the back. She carefully opened it taking care not to rip the envelope and slipped out a card with gold edging.

Just as was her mother-in-law Lucy, back in 1910, Anna was stunned and excited. She couldn't wait for Jack to get home so she could tell him the news. She started to plan her wardrobe but soon realised nothing would be suitable. A shopping trip to Oxford Street would need to be undertaken.

Jack walked in the door at about six and Anna nearly bowled him over, throwing her arms around his neck and jabbering something about the King and Queen.

'Whoa, hold on honey! What's going on?'

'We're going to meet the King and Queen. At a garden party! At Buckingham Palace. I'm so excited!'

Anna showed Jack the invitation.

'Honey that's wonderful, but the chances of actually meeting the King and Queen are pretty slim. There's going to be lots of people there.

'I don't care, there's a chance. Besides, how many people do you know who've sipped tea at Buckingham Palace?'

150

'Not many I must admit.'

'I'm going shopping for a new outfit on Saturday. I think I'll take Bridget with me – she knows all the best shops.'

And so it was for the next few weeks; all conversation at the dinner table revolved around the Royal garden party.

Finally the day came and at 3.30 pm an Embassy motor vehicle, a black Buick Phaeton, arrived at the Savoy. Anna looked stunning in her Norman Hartnell outfit and together with Jack in his Brigadier's uniform they looked the perfect American couple.

They showed their ticket at the gate and walked into the magnificent gardens with white marquees and fountains shooting streams of water into the air.

Initially they were not sure what to do, but then Anna spotted Harry and Julie. They quickly walked over and after the normal greetings agreed they should enter one of the marquees and avail themselves of a cup of tea and a dainty sandwiches.

Jack and Anna had been at the garden party about an hour when Harry sighted George and Elizabeth mingling with their guests.

> 'Well Anna, here's your chance to meet the King and Queen,' Harry said jovially. 'They are very nice people I can assure you. Very friendly.'
>
> 'What! You've met them?'
>
> 'Oh yes, a number of times actually. So has Julie. One of the benefits of owning a title.'
>
> 'You've never mentioned it to us before. Why not?' Anna inquired.
>
> 'I don't know. Didn't think you would be that interested.'
>
> 'I' don't believe you Harry - you English are so laid back!'

While this conversation was taking place the King and Queen had moved closer to the group. Before they knew it, Jack and Anna were shaking the hands of the British monarchs.

King George inquired about Jack's reason for being in London. When Jack explained that he was the Military Attaché his ears pricked up.

> 'Brigadier Doherty today is not the time, but I would be very interested in hearing your views about the war in Europe and

America's attitude. Would you be so kind as to contact my office on Monday and arrange a mutually suitable time to talk?'

'Yes your Majesty. Of course.'

'Splendid! I look forward to seeing you again shortly. Ask for Major the Rt Hon. Sir Alexander Hardinge. He is my secretary and will arrange things.'

Meantime Queen Elizabeth chatted to Anna and Julie, not about the weather or the gardens but about living in London during wartime.

The weather had been perfect and so had the day. Anna spoke with the Queen and Jack would have the same opportunity to brief the King, as did his father before him.

During the war, King George and Queen Elizabeth remained in London for most of the time, at Buckingham Palace (the Palace was bombed nine times during the war). The Royal couple visited severely bombed areas in the East End of London and elsewhere in the country. This gained them great popularity.

The King developed a close working relationship with his wartime Prime Minister, Winston Churchill, as most of Europe fell to Nazi Germany.

# 33. By George, I Think He's Got It!

As was required, Jack informed the Under Secretary of the Navy of his intended meeting with King George VI. Gene saw no problem with it; in fact, he encouraged Jack to be open and frank with the King.

On the Monday after his chance encounter with the King Jack called the palace and spoke with Major Hardinge. A suitable time was arranged: Jack would meet with the King on the following Monday morning 25th November at 11 am.

The Embassy car, a Lincoln Continental this time, drove Brigadier Doherty to Buckingham Palace for his meeting with King George. As with his father, the King's secretary Major Hardinge met him.

He was led down the same magnificent hall to enter the King's private office. He recalled his father's description of the King's office; it was just as his father had described years earlier:

> 'It was not just an office. It was quite large and had bookcases on three sides. It overlooked some magnificent gardens. Various priceless paintings adorned the walls and the desk was something to behold - an eighteenth-century Chippendale originally made for King George III.'

Brigadier Doherty was invited to sit on the leather lounge and wait for the King to appear. He didn't have to wait too long when George VI entered his office and shook the hand of the American officer.

> 'Brigadier, I appreciate your taking the time out of what I am sure is a very busy schedule.'

> 'It is my pleasure, your Majesty.'

> 'I am naturally very concerned about how this God-awful European war is going. We are being stretched to the limit as you probably already know and Hitler seems to be making gain after gain.'

> 'I can assure you, your Majesty, President Roosevelt is extremely concerned and is trying to help as much as he can. Having said that,

he and the American people have no desire to enter into another European war. We are still licking our wounds from the last one.'

'Mr Churchill informs me that you have undertaken some actions that seems to be hurting Hitler and his allies, the Japanese.'

'That's true. We have embargoed oil, denying Japan fuel. It's estimated that they have about one month's supply remaining.'

'Wouldn't that force them into invading countries to secure more supplies?'

'We believe our embargo will in fact prevent the Japanese from attacking your oil-rich territory in East Asia i.e. Malaya and Singapore, and Holland's Indonesia. Are you aware of the terms of the 'Lend Lease Program', your Majesty?'

**Roosevelt Signing the Lend-Lease Bill**

'I am aware that we are receiving loans from America to help us and our allies purchase much needed weapons.'

'America has so far lent Britain and its allies close to fifteen billion dollars. A total of $50.1 billion worth of supplies were shipped. That represented 17 percent of the total war expenditures of the US. In all, $31.4 billion went to Britain, $11.3 billion to the Soviet Union, $3.2 billion to France, $1.6 billion to China, and smaller sums to other Allies. Reverse Lend-Lease comprised services such as rent on air bases that went to the US, and totalled $7.8 billion; of this, $6.8 billion came from the British and the Commonwealth.'

Jack continued, 'Additionally on 2nd September 1940, President Roosevelt signed a 'Destroyers for Bases' agreement with Britain. Under the terms of this agreement, the United States will give you more than fifty decommissioned destroyers, in exchange for ninety-nine year leases in Newfoundland and the Caribbean, which will be used as US air and naval bases.

'Your Prime Minister, Winston Churchill originally requested that Mr Roosevelt provide the destroyers as a gift, but our President knew that the American people and the Congress would oppose such a deal. So, it can be said that America fully supports your war effort.'

'You don't think America will enter the war, unless it is attacked?'

'No, your Majesty, however President Roosevelt had given orders that any German ship found in the eastern Atlantic should be fired on and sunk. This means to a certain extent, the United States has more or less entered the War of the Atlantic. We are determined to keep Britain's sea routes safe.'

'It is an uncertain world we live in Brigadier. Are you prepared if by chance you are forced into the war?'

'We are. The US Army has grown massively from 267,767 personnel in 1940 to 1,460,998 currently.'

'We as a nation appreciate America's help, Brigadier.'

'The American people fully support you. In fact, 83 percent of Americans want Britain and France to win the war against Germany.'

'Really? Not one hundred percent?'

'Well, considering 17 percent of our population is of German decent it's a pretty high figure.'

'I see. Hhmm. Yes, you are right.'

The King thanked Jack for his honesty and his time and bid him farewell.

When he returned to his office Jack began to write his report to the Under Secretary of the Navy.

# 34.Chop Chop

## Off We Go

Jack and Anna were enjoying their time in London despite Britain being at war with Germany. There had been no bombing raids to date and they got to spend time with Julie and Harry. The weekend stays at Raby Castle were wonderful - Jack and Harry would inevitably go hunting and on occasion Julie and Anna would join them. The boys were most indignant when Anna bagged a magnificent stag. Harry agreed to have the antlers mounted and send them down to London so she could claim boasting rights.

On one such weekend Harry broached the subject of Asia with Jack.

'Jack, keep this under your hat, but I have been approached to head up the Government's Health Department in South East Asia. We would be based in Singapore. It is a big job but the Minister for Health thinks I'm up to it.

'Why would you want to go half way around the world for a Government position? Surely you and Julie have everything you could possibly want right here?'

'That's just it. I am privileged by birthright but have not really achieved anything under my own name. I want to make a contribution.'

'What does Julie think?'

'She's all for it. It would only be for five years then we're back here continuing our work and lifestyle. By then I'm sure this bloody war will be over and Hitler will either be dead or sitting in a cold dungeon somewhere waiting to be hanged.'

'We both loved Singapore when we visited on our honeymoon, and the rest of the region is amazing.

'Will Julie be able to continue her work?'

'Oh yes! She would be responsible for plastic surgery and the burns unit. She's quite looking forward to it.'

'So what advice do you want from me?'

156

'Well, with this bloody war going on in Europe we feel we would be safer in Asia. The point is my man, Julie is pregnant and we would rather have a baby in a country that is unlikely to be invaded. The Government wants us to go - who are we to argue? The advice I seek from you is this - is Japan likely to move on from China and create bedlam through out Asia?'

'To be perfectly honest, nobody predicted Japan invading Manchuria. When they did, we thought they would depart in a year. They have been there four years and from what little intelligence we have been able to gather they are wreaking havoc. The big issue for you two is how safe is Singapore? It is a fortress island. Winston Churchill calls it "The Gibraltar of the East". It will be protected by the pride of the British Navy. If you were to go anywhere in Asia it would have to be Singapore.'

'Thank you Jack! That's what I wanted to hear.'

'When are you thinking of going?'

'In two months if we can sort out a caretaker for the castle and the manor. The current caretakers look like they will accept the positions.'

'I'll keep you posted on any developments I hear about.'

# 35.Adventure in the Far East

## 1st August 1939

Julie and Harry were finally prepared for their sea voyage to Singapore. They had been successful in arranging staff and management for their two properties, Raby Castle and Westmoreland Manor. They were to sail on the newly constructed RMS *Mauretania* in first class; the voyage would take six weeks.

CUNARD R.M.S. MAURETANIA 35,674 TONS.

1290      CUNARD WHITE STAR LINER      34.000 Tons
C. R. Hoffmann,      "MAURETANIA."
Southampton.      CABIN GRAND HALL

The voyage went without incident and the ship's facilities were second to none.

1285 C. R. Hoffmann,      CUNARD WHITE STAR LINER   "MAURETANIA,"      34.000 Tons
Southampton.      THIRD CLASS LOUNGE

# Singapore

It is unknown when Singapore was first settled.

A third century Chinese account describes it as *Pu-luo-chung*, or the 'island at the end of a peninsula'. Later, the city was known as Temasek ('Sea Town'), when the first settlements were established in AD 1298.

During the 14$^{th}$ century this small but strategically located island was renamed. According to legend, Sang Nila Utama, a Prince from Palembang (the capital of Srivijaya), was out on a hunting trip when he caught sight of an animal he had never seen before. Taking it to be a good sign, he founded a city where the animal had been spotted, naming it 'The Lion City' or *Singapura*, from the Sanskrit words *simha* (lion) and *pura* (city).

The five kings of ancient Singapura then ruled the city. Located at the tip of the Malay Peninsula, the natural meeting point of sea routes, the city served as a flourishing trading post for a wide variety of sea vessels, including Chinese junks, Indian vessels, Arab dhows, Portuguese battleships, and Buginese schooners from Indonesia.

The next important period in the history of Singapore was during the 19$^{th}$ century, when modern Singapore was founded. At this time, Singapore was already an up-and-coming trading post along the Malacca Straits. It was also then that Great Britain started to see the need for a port of call in the region. In particular, British traders needed a strategic venue to base the merchant fleet of the growing Empire, and to forestall any advance made by the Dutch in the region.

The then Lieutenant-Governor of Bengkulu in Sumatra, Sir Thomas Stamford Raffles, landed in Singapore on 29$^{th}$ January 1819 after a survey of the neighbouring islands. Recognising the immense potential of the swamp-covered island, he helped negotiate a treaty with the local rulers and established Singapore as a trading station. Soon, the island's policy of free trade attracted merchants from all over Asia and from as far away as the Middle East and the US.

In 1832, Singapore became the centre of government for the Straits Settlements of Penang, Malacca and Singapore. With the opening of the Suez Canal in 1869 and the advent of the telegraph and steamship, Singapore's importance as a centre of the expanding trade between the East and West increased tremendously between 1873 and 1913. Its prosperity attracted immigrants from around the region. By 1860, the thriving island nation had a population that had grown from one hundred and fifty in 1819 to eighty one thousand, comprising mainly Chinese, Indians and Malays.

After the First World War, the British government devoted significant resources to building a naval base in Singapore, as a deterrent to the increasingly ambitious Japanese Empire. Originally announced in 1923, the construction of the base proceeded slowly until the Japanese invasion of Manchuria in 1931. When completed in 1939, at the very significant cost of five hundred million dollars, it boasted what was then the largest dry dock in the world, the third-largest floating dock, and enough fuel tanks to support the entire British Navy for six months. Heavy 15-inch naval guns stationed at Fort Siloso, Fort Canning and Labrador, as well as a Royal Air Force airfield at Tengah Air Base defended it. Winston Churchill touted it as the 'Gibraltar of the East.'

Unfortunately, it was a base without a fleet. The British Home Fleet was stationed in Europe, and the British could not afford to build a second fleet to protect its interests in Asia. The plan was for the Home Fleet to sail quickly to Singapore in the event of an emergency.

**Singapore Harbour 1942**

161

# 36. The Good Life

## Shall we meet at Raffles or the Tanglin Club?

The Secretary to the Governor of Singapore, Major John Lipett met Harry and Julie at the wharf. Once their luggage had been retrieved and they cleared customs they were driven to their new home close to the hospital.

They were both used to living in luxury back in England but they thought they would be living more modestly in Singapore. This was not to be so – they were allocated a magnificent Singapore mansion, with ten servants, in the best location on the island.

The Head of Health Services for the Straits Settlements was a respected position in Singapore according many privileges. One of those privileges was membership of the exclusive Tanglin Club where they would meet their friends for tennis and drinks on the deck.

Harry and Julie were keen to see the hospital and made that their first visit the following day. They didn't have to worry about unpacking - the servants took care of everything.

A driver was waiting for them at nine am as arranged, driving them to the Alexandra Military Hospital otherwise known as the British Military Hospital. The medical facility had been established in 1938 as the primary military hospital four miles west of Singapore at 378 Alexandra Road, hence its common name.

The Alexandra Military Hospital served as the principal hospital for the British Far East Command and was an institution that adopted cutting-edge medical technology.

The two doctors inspected the wards, chatting to young soldiers and sailors who had suffered life-changing injuries. The operating theatres were of particular interest and both were impressed with the equipment and the sophistication of the theatres.

The next appointment was to visit the Governor of Singapore, Sir Cecil Clementi.

**Sir Cecil Clementi**

The Governor welcomed the husband and wife medical team to Government House where they drank tea on the veranda overlooking the magnificent tropical gardens. Sir Cecil knew Harry's parents and was aware of their tragic deaths. He reminisced about the times he had spent at Raby Castle. Julie had continued to be amazed at Harry's social network ever since she met Dame Nellie Melba at her farewell concert.

Sir Cecil confided his great concern relating to the threat of imperialist Japan to South East Asia and particularly Singapore and Malaya.

'Do you really think they would try and take Singapore? Churchill calls it the Gibraltar of the East,' asked Harry.

'I don't mean to question Mr Churchill's strategy but it does rely on an invasion from the sea. All our big guns are pointing out to the Singapore Straits. If the Japanese decide to invade through Malaya we have no real defence,' said Sir Cecil.

'Well, I hope Churchill is right although from what I hear from my military chums the Japanese would be no match for the

Commonwealth forces. They may have been able to knock off the Chinese but Britain is another kettle of fish altogether,' said Harry.

'I hope you're right Harry, for all our sakes.'

Harry and Julie bade their farewells and returned to their house where the servants were preparing the evening meal. The house came with its own substantial wine cellar - Harry was looking forward to his first inspection and selection.

Life in Singapore centred on their medical responsibilities and their social life. The British and Australian expatriates made them more than welcome and invitations to dinner or drinks were abundant.

Julie's favourite pastime outside of the hospital was visiting the Tanglin Club. The Olympic-sized pool and tennis court gave her much pleasure, as did the Singapore golf club.

# 25<sup>th</sup> December 1939

The de Nevilles were invited to Government House for a traditional Christmas dinner although with the temperature outside pushing one hundred and the humidity around ninety percent it was hardly the traditional weather they were used to.

Lieutenant-General Arthur Percival and his wife were also guests, as well as Air Chief Marshal Sir Robert Brooke-Popham, the Commander-in-Chief of the British Far East Command, and his wife. The remainder of the table consisted of high-ranking British public servants and various business people.

As to be expected the dinner conversation concentrated on what was happening in Europe.

'What have you heard about the Russians invading Finland, Arthur?'

'Well, Sir Robert, the latest information we have is that the Bolshies have bombed Helsinki and the Finns have retreated to the Mannerheim Line.'

'They have no hope of holding them back.'

'No, I am afraid you're right,' agreed Arthur.

Another guest, David Meyer, joined the conversation.

'Are you surprised, gentlemen, that Italy has declared its neutrality? It is my understanding that Norway, Sweden, and Denmark have also proclaimed their neutrality leaving the Finns to battle Russia on her own.'

'Not at all, David. No-one wants to take on the Russians if they don't have to.'

'I suppose you're right Sir Robert.'

'News came in just today that the destroyer HMS *Duchess* has sunk after a collision with the battleship HMS *Barham* off the coast of Scotland with the loss of one hundred and twenty-four men.'

'For God's sake! We have enough trouble avoiding the German's U-Boats without sinking our own!'

'That's terrible news, Sir Robert. Those poor men and their families,' said Julie with real concern.

A lone piper piping in the beef silenced the conversation around the table. The Chinese servants brought in the magnificent Christmas dinner; not only the beef but also turkey and ham, with platters of vegetables grown in the Governor's own vegetable garden. Arthur Percival encouraged everybody to enjoy the meal and to give a thought to those back home who were on severe rations.

After the main course was cleared the servants arrived with a large Christmas pudding together with silver custard boats and fresh cream. Every one of the guests requested a second helping.

The Governor suggested they retire to the veranda for coffee and port and they all duly followed him.

'I know we have been discussing Europe, understandably so, as we have a war going on over there, but what about here? The Japanese are virtually on our doorstep,' commented Major Terrence Joyce Adjutant to Lieutenant-General Arthur Percival.

'There is very little chance Major, that Japan could penetrate our naval and land-based defences. Britain would never concede Singapore and Malaya.' Percival spoke with conviction.

The other guests on the veranda on that hot and humid Christmas Day nodded in agreement with Percival.

**Governor's Residence**

The conversations continued until midnight when the first of the cars arrived to take them back to their residences. All in all it had been a wonderful Christmas dinner.

# 37. A Fortunate Life

## Singapore 1<sup>st</sup> January 1940

Harry and Julie joined a group of friends at Raffles Hotel to celebrate the New Year. They all wore party hats and drank the Veuve Clicquot which had been placed on every table. A Chinese big band played all night and the mood was one of optimism for the coming year.

## April 1940

Julie gave birth to an eight-pound baby girl. Harry and Julie name her Lara after Harry's grandmother.

## Europe May 1940

10<sup>th</sup> May

German paratroopers land in The Hague and Rotterdam.

10<sup>th</sup> May

German airborne elements land across Belgium and Holland in advance of ground forces, capturing key bridges and routes.

10<sup>th</sup> May

Eighty-nine German paratroopers land and take the Belgium fortress of Eben Emael with its garrison of two thousand soldiers.

11<sup>th</sup> May

British and French army forces begin defensive preparations in Belgium in an effort to stave off the German advance. A long line of strategic defences is constructed.

14<sup>th</sup> May

Facing light opposition, German Panzer Corps XV, XLI and XIX are free to set up three key bridgeheads covering Dinant, Montherme and Sedan.

14<sup>th</sup> May

Panzer Corps XV and XIX break through the Allied defences at Sedan, allowing German forces to completely bypass the formidable defences at the French Maginot Line.

15<sup>th</sup> May

German Panzer Corps cross into the north of France.

15<sup>th</sup> May

After periods of heavy bombing all across Rotterdam, the Dutch surrender to the Germans.

15<sup>th</sup> May

The RAF sends up its first night time bombing raid against Germany. Of the ninety-nine aircraft sent, only one fails to return home.

17<sup>th</sup> – 18<sup>th</sup> May

Allied forces are in full retreat of the Germans, making their way towards the French coastline.

17<sup>th</sup> – 18<sup>th</sup> May

Antwerp falls to the German Army.

17<sup>th</sup> – 18<sup>th</sup> May

Brussels falls to the German Army.

20<sup>th</sup> May

Sensing a catastrophic loss in the making, Winston Churchill orders preparation of vessels to evacuate the British Expeditionary Forces from northern France.

20th May

Compounding battlefield losses across France and the Low Countries, the Allies implement a change at the top. French General, Maxime Weygand replaces General Maurice-Gustave Gamelin as Supreme Allied Commander.

21st May

An Allied counterattack against the German Army near Arras ends in failure, as the attack is itself countered by another advancing German land force.

24th May

German Luftwaffe bombers hammer Allied defensive positions in and around the French port city of Dunkirk.

24th May

In a stunning move, Hitler orders his forces not to cross the Lens-Bethune-St Omer-Gravelines, allowing the retreating Allied forces more time to reach the French coast.

25th May

The German Army takes Boulogne.

25th May

Retreating Allied units arrive at the French port city of Dunkirk.

26th May

Over eight hundred and fifty British civilian vessels take part in assisting military forces to retreat from French soil. This would become the largest military evacuation in history.

26th May

Hitler orders his army forces towards Dunkirk for the final blow to the Allies.

26th May

Operation Dynamo, the all-out evacuation of Allied forces from Dunkirk officially begins.

28th May

The Belgian Army surrenders to the German 6th and 18th armies. This action gives the evacuating forces more time.

28th May

With Belgium now out of the war, the German Army begins making its way towards the French coastline in an attempt to completely destroy the Allied forces.

28th May

By the end of this historical day, twenty-five thousand four hundred and seventy-three British soldiers have been evacuated from France.

29th May

Another forty-seven thousand British troops are evacuated from Dunkirk.

30th May

A further six thousand French soldiers join an additional one hundred and twenty thousand Allied soldiers to be evacuated from Dunkirk.

31st May

Over one hundred and fifty thousand Allied soldiers arrive in Britain.

# Singapore May 1940

10th May

Harry and Julie attend a surprise fancy dress party for their good friend's fortieth birthday. They dressed as pirates. The Nanny cares for Lara.

11th May

Drinks and dinner at the Tanglin Club.

17<sup>th</sup> May

Dinner at the Bowes' villa in Bukit Timah.

24<sup>th</sup> May

Tennis at dusk at the Tanglin Club followed by dinner.

25<sup>th</sup> May

Foursomes Golf at the Royal Tanglin Golf Course, then dinner.

31<sup>st</sup> May

Julie and Harry attended a performance of *Swan Lake* at the Singapore Dance Theatre.

On all the other days in May the two doctors went about their duties operating on various patients, including soldiers severely injured in training exercises. The Nanny had a busy month.

The month of May brought different experiences to both Europe and Singapore. However the winds of change were blowing across the Singapore Straits.

# 38. War over There

## Singapore Slings Over Here

## Singapore 1941

Harry and Julie spent their time between the various hospitals and health clinics. Being the senior surgeons on the island required them to practise general as well as plastic surgery. Although they were not required to reconstruct faces after horrific war injuries they did perform some critical procedures. These were usually as a result of accidents on the wharves and plantations.

As part of their responsibilities, trips to Malaya and Hong Kong were undertaken twice a year. This they both enjoyed, not just for medical reasons, but also because it gave them an opportunity to meet with expatriates from various parts of the world. There were doctors from Australia, New Zealand, Canada and South Africa, all working to improve the health of their patients.

Conversations over a gin and tonic invariably would include the Japanese threat although most believed Churchill and felt safe in their British utopia.

Julie's brother Jack wasn't enjoying the same relaxed lifestyle in England. There was a serious war going on.

## London May 1941

Jack Doherty was sitting at his desk in the American Headquarters in London. He had recently been promoted to a One Star General and as a result, commanded his own office with a briefing room attached - not quite the command he had hoped for.

Jack's career in the Marines had centred on intelligence; he knew the importance of information and the power it could give. A war could be won or lost based on the level of intelligence each side could accumulate on their enemy's movements or plans.

He received a telephone call from Gene Lutze, the Under Secretary of the Navy and his mother's second husband.

'Jack, it's Gene. Are you alone?'

'Is your telephone line secure?

'Yes Gene. Why do you ask?'

'I've got some very confidential news. Could turn the course of the war.'

'My God! What is it?'

'One of the Enigma machines used by the German Navy has been acquired from a captured U-Boat. If we can determine how it works we will be able to decipher the coded messages being sent. We believe the Polish and British are close to breaking the code on the primary Enigma. If we can break both, it would put us in a very strong position. The British command has requested your involvement and I have agreed. I want you to move to Bletchley Park in Buckinghamshire - by the end of this week.'

'Yes sir. Who do I pass on working files to while I'm gone?'

'Don't worry about that. I'll appoint someone worthy and capable to continue your work. You could well be back in your office before you know it.'

'Gene, where will I sit as far as level of command?'

'You will remain reporting to me but the British officer heading up the operation is Commander Alastair Denniston. He's the number one British code-breaker. He heads up the Government Code and Cypher School (GC&CS). The British certainly come up with some strange names.'

'You mentioned the Polish - how come they are involved?'

'The Germans, specifically Albert Scherbius, invented the Enigma back in 1919. It was patented and further developed by the company Gewerkschaft Securitas after they purchased the patents from Scherbius. The German armed forces initially rejected Enigma but eventually saw merit in adopting it for encrypting messages.

'The Polish customs service discovered one being smuggled into the German Embassy in Warsaw. They embarked on a program of re-engineering to determine how the machine worked. Determining the exact wiring of each of the three rotors became the Polish cryptanalysts' first task. To accomplish this, Poland's cypher bureau tested and hired three mathematicians in 1932: Marian

Rejewski, Jerzy Rozycki, and Henryk Zygalski. They painstakingly analysed the intercepted encrypted messages searching for clues. Rejewski eventually determined a mathematical equation that could determine the wiring connections. However, the equation had too many unknown variables. He was able to finally make the initial breaks into the wiring sequence only with the aid of a German traitor.'

'So how did the British get involved, Gene?'

'On 25th July 1939, in Warsaw, the Poles initiated French and British military intelligence representatives into their Enigma-decryption techniques and equipment, including the Zygalski sheets and the cryptologic bombe, and promised each delegation a Polish-reconstructed Enigma machine. Without these gifts of techniques and technology from Polish military intelligence, decryption of German Enigma messages at Bletchley Park would not have been possible.

'Well, it sounds like an incredible project sir. I hope I can make a contribution. I am sure once I am ensconced at Bletchley Park I will have a better understanding of the challenges ahead.'

# 39. What Did He Say?

**Bletchley Park**

When Jack arrived at BP as everyone called Bletchley Park, he was impressed with the grand manor house set in beautiful gardens. 'I can work here', he thought.

He entered the main entrance, a gothic structure with a griffin on either side guarding the doors to the impressive foyer. At the reception desk sat a very pretty young lady, one of the ten thousand who were either working, or had worked, at Bletchley Park during project 'Ultra'.

'Good morning, my name is General Doherty of the United States Marines. I have an appointment with Commander Denniston.'

'Yes sir. I'll let his secretary know you are here.'

A tall man who looked more like a university professor than a commander entered the waiting room.

'Hello General. Alastair Denniston,' said the commander, extending his arm to shake hands rather than salute.

'Good morning, Commander.'

'Please, we are very informal here. Have to be really. Some of the brightest people working on this project are civilians. Now, would you like a tour of our establishment, Jack?'

'Thank you Alastair. I'm real keen to see what you are up to.'

Commander Alastair Denniston was Operational Head of GC&CS from its formation out of the Admiralty's Room 40 and the War Office's MI1B in 1919, until 1942. On the day that Britain declared war on Germany, he wrote to the Foreign Office about recruiting 'men of the 'intellectual type'.

Personal networking was used for the initial recruitment, particularly from the universities of Cambridge, Oxford, and Aberdeen. Reliable and trustworthy women to perform administrative and clerical tasks were similarly recruited by personal contacts. This has been characterised as recruiting 'Boffins and Debs' or 'Dilly's Fillies' (Dilly Knox), and the indexing section where many of the women worked was called 'The Deb's Delight'.

Cryptanalysts were selected for various intellectual achievements, whether they were linguists, chess champions, crossword experts, polyglots or great mathematicians. GC&CS was ironically referred to as 'the Golf, Cheese and Chess Society'. In one instance, the ability to solve a *Daily Telegraph* crossword in less than twelve minutes was used as a test. The newspaper was asked to organise a competition, after which each of the successful participants was contacted and asked whether they would be prepared to undertake 'a particular type of work as a contribution to the war effort'. FHW Hawes of Dagenham in Essex finished in less than eight minutes and won the competition itself.

New entrants were given a basic grounding in code-breaking at the Inter-Service Special Intelligence School set up by John Tiltman. Initially at an RAF depot in Buckingham, it moved to an ex-Gas Company showroom in Ardour House, 1 Albany Road, Bedford, which was known locally as the 'Spy School'.

Working in three shifts or 'watches' over twenty-four hours was inaugurated by the Air Section in Hut 10 under Josh Cooper, and the practice soon became universal. The shifts were 4 pm to midnight, midnight to 8 am and 8 am to 4 pm Staff had a six-day week, and rotated through the three shifts. Thirty minutes was allowed for the meal in the middle of the shift.

The irregular working hours affected workers' health and social life, and the private homes nearby where most staff was billeted. The work was tedious and required concentration, some 'girls' collapsed and required extended rest. The staff got one-week's leave four times a year.

Nine thousand armed services personnel and civilians were working at Bletchley Park at the height of the code-breaking project in January 1945 and over twelve thousand worked there at some point during the war, eighty percent of them women. A relatively small number of men were also employed on a part-time basis, typically for one shift each week when they were used for their Morse code or knowledge of the German language.

Key cryptanalysts included

# John Tiltman

Tiltman was an early and persistent advocate of British cooperation with the United States in cryptology. In 1944, he was promoted to Brigadier and appointed Deputy Director of GC&CS. He continued in 1946, as Assistant Director of the Government Communications Headquarters (GCHQ), successor to GC&CS. He retired as a Brigadier

# Dillwyn 'Dilly' Knox

Dilly developed a system known as 'rodding', a linguistic as opposed to mathematical way of breaking codes. This technique worked on the Enigma used by the Italian Navy and the German Abwehr, the German intelligence unit. Knox worked in the 'Cottage', next door to the Bletchley Park mansion, as head of a research section, which contributed significantly to cryptanalysis of the Enigma.

Knox's team at the Cottage used rodding to decrypt intercepted Italian naval signals describing the sailing of an Italian battle fleet, leading to The Battle of Cape Matapan. Admiral John Godfrey, Director of Naval Intelligence credited the Allied victory at Matapan to this intelligence.

# Gordon Welchman

Just before World War II, Welchman, an American, was invited by Commander Alastair Denniston to join the Government Code & Cypher School at Bletchley

Park, in case war broke out. He was one of four early recruits to Bletchley and made significant contribution to the 'Ultra' project.

# Alan Turing

Turing is widely considered to be the father of computer science and artificial intelligence.

Turing worked for the GC&CS at Bletchley Park. For a time he was head of Hut 8, the section responsible for German naval cryptanalysis. He devised a number of techniques for breaking German cyphers, including the method of the bombe, an electromechanical machine that could find settings for the Enigma machine.

# Hugh Alexander

In February 1940, Alexander arrived at Bletchley Park and joined Hut 6, the section tasked with breaking German Army and Air Force Enigma messages. In 1941, he transferred to Hut 8, the corresponding hut working on Naval Enigma messages. He became Deputy Head of Hut 8 under Alan Turing. Alexander was more involved with the day-to-day operations of the hut than Turing, and, while

Turing was visiting the United States, Alexander formally became the Head of Hut 8.

Other key players included:

Harry Hinsley

John Jeffreys

Peter Twinn

Stuart Milner-Barry

**Hut 8**

# 40. Enigma

*'A person or thing that is mysterious or difficult to understand.'*

Jack and Alastair made their way out of Bletchley Park's main entrance walking down a gravel path with timber huts on either side.

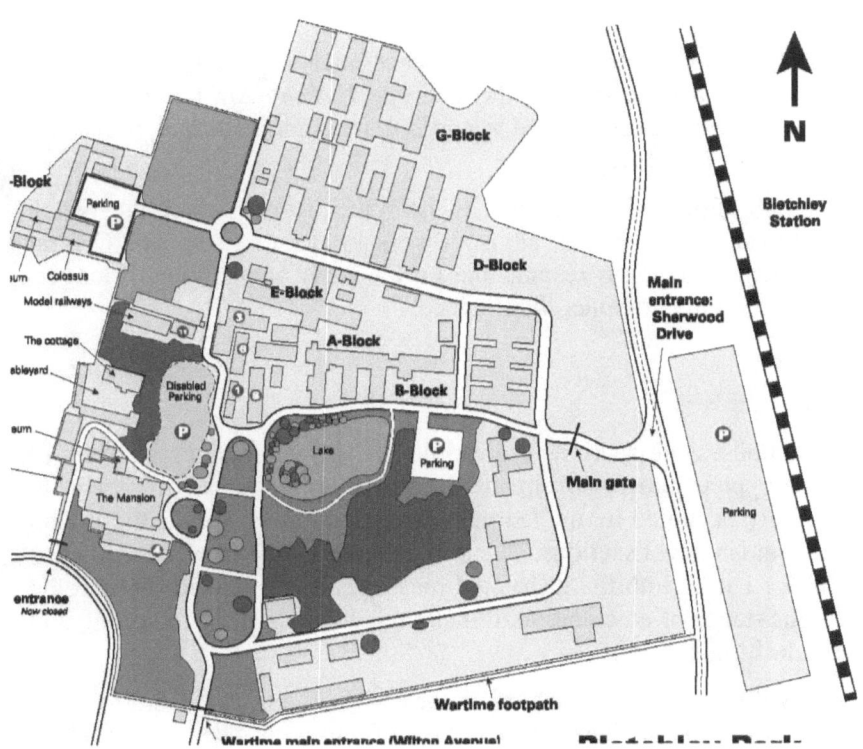

**Bletchley Park's Grounds**

'As you can see, Jack, the grandiose mansion overshadows the huts where the actual work is done. Let me briefly explain what is taking place in each hut.'

Hut 1

Function:

'We have developed our first bombe (computer) in there. We aptly called it 'Victory'. This is where Alan Turing and Gordon Welchman weaved their magic initially. I will introduce you later on.'

HUT 2

Function:

Recreation Hut, serving provisions and luncheon vouchers.

HUT 3

Function:

'Hut 3 is responsible for the intelligence analysis through translation, emendation and sorting of the decrypted Army/Air Force material from Hut 6. It's disseminated to appropriate commands and ministries, and to units in the field.

'The hub of operations in Hut 3 is the Watch Room, where the Watch and Naval, Army and Air advisors work in close liaison. The Central Intelligence Section is responsible for the study and solving of longer-term and highly complex intelligence.'

HUT 4

Function:

Hut 4 houses the section responsible for the intelligence analysis of the decrypted material from the German Navy sourced from Hut 8. Currently occupied by the German naval section as well as the Italian and Spanish naval sections. The processes of Hut 4 are very similar to those of Hut 3 with the decrypted messages being passed through the various stages of emendation, translation, evaluation, commenting and sign drafting.

'We will look at the other huts tomorrow, Jack, but I do want to show you Hut 8. That's where you will be working with Alan Turing. He is a brilliant fellow. He's been working on the naval Enigma which by all accounts is the most difficult to crack. He has developed the most advanced bombe to date. I am sure he would be more than happy to demonstrate it to you.'

Alistair and Jack entered Hut 8. It was a hive of activity with WRENs (Women's Royal Naval Service) everywhere typing and analysing documents.

**Hut 8 Bletchley Park**

Alistair approached a man with a shaggy tweed coat and hair that could only be described as unkempt.

'Hello Alan, I would like you to meet General Jack Doherty. He's been assigned to 'Ultra' to assist your project with anything America can provide.'

'Pleased to meet you, General.'

'Please call me Jack. Yes, the President and the Under Secretary of the Navy have made it very clear to me that I should do anything I can to assist you.'

'That's nice. Would you like to see our baby?'

'Baby?'

'Our Bombe, General.'

'Oh, of course. Yes! I would love a demonstration.'

'Follow me.'

Turing led them through to another room attached to the hut. There, sitting proudly with its cogs spinning and whirring was Turing's bombe.

**Turing's Bombe**

'So, here she is, the machine that is cracking the naval Enigma codes and putting German U-boats where they belong - on the bottom of the ocean,' boasted Turing.

'I'm not a mathematician by any stretch of the imagination Alan, but it does look impressive. How can we help?'

'You have a company in America. NCR. I believe this company could build a bombe to our specifications, yet still improve on our design.'

Jack returned to the United States in April 1942 and while there visited the US Navy cryptanalysis office.

At his meeting with the Under Secretary he stressed the importance of tracking German U-Boat traffic. He highlighted the urgent need for an Enigma-cracking machine. Jack divulged his doubts about the size of the British engineering workload resulting in slow progress. He prompted the US to start investigating designs for a Navy bombe, based on the full blueprints and wiring diagrams received by US Naval Lieutenants Robert Ely and Joseph Eachus at Bletchley Park in July 1942.

Funding for two million dollars for a Navy development effort was requested on 3$^{rd}$ September 1942. It was approved the following day.

The US Navy Bombe contained sixteen four-rotor Enigma-analogues and was much faster than the British three-rotor bombes, even for a three-rotor task.

Commander Edward Travis, Deputy Director and Frank Birch, Head of the German Naval Section travelled from Bletchley Park to Washington in September 1942. With Carl Frederick Holden, US Director of Naval Communications they established, on 2nd October 1942, a UK US accord. This established a relationship of 'full collaboration' between Bletchley Park and OP-20-G.

An all-electronic solution to the problem of a fast bombe was considered but rejected for pragmatic reasons, and a contract was let with the National Cash Register Corporation (NCR) in Dayton, Ohio. This established the United States Naval Computing Machine Laboratory.

Jack returned to Bletchley Park continuing his high level collaboration with his British counterparts. Over the next few years they achieved great results saving the lives of thousands of Allied forces.

# 41.Planning the D-Day Invasion

**Stalin, Roosevelt and Churchill**

President Roosevelt was feeling shattered after the seven thousand-mile journey to Tehran to meet with Winston Churchill and Joseph Stalin.

He suffered from polio, which confined him to a wheelchair for most of the time, but it was not this condition that taxed his energy levels; it was cardiovascular disease consisting of congestive heart failure, hypertension, and hypertensive heart disease. It was this condition that would lead to his death less than eighteen months later.

The conference was scheduled to convene at 16:00 on 28th November 1943. Stalin arrived early, followed by Roosevelt, who was wheeled in.

Churchill, strolling and smoking his signature cigar, arrived half an hour later.

The two major western powers had agreed that their main objective was to ensure full cooperation and assistance from the Soviet Union for their war policies. Stalin agreed, but with conditions: Stalin pressed for a revision of Poland's eastern border with the Soviet Union to match the line set by British Foreign Secretary Lord Curzon in 1920. In order to compensate Poland for the resulting loss of territory, the three leaders agreed to move the German-Polish border to the Oder and Neisse rivers.

Roosevelt, Churchill, and Stalin then moved on to other more important matters, namely the cross-Channel invasion of occupied France by the Western Allies (Operation Overlord) and general war policy. Operation Overlord was scheduled to begin in May 1944, in conjunction with a Soviet attack on Germany's eastern border.

Roosevelt gave Stalin a pledge that he had been waiting for since June 1941: that the British and the Americans would open a second front in France in the spring of 1944. Churchill up to this point had been seeking a joint United Kingdom, United States and Commonwealth forces initiative through the Mediterranean that would have secured British interests in the Middle East and India. The three leaders agreed that the nations in league with the Axis powers would be divided into territories to be controlled by the Soviet Union, the US, and the UK.

Iran and Turkey were discussed in detail; they all agreed to support Iran's government, as addressed in the following declaration:

> The Three Governments realise that the war has caused special economic difficulties for Iran, and they all agreed that they will continue to make available to the Government of Iran such economic assistance as may be possible, having regard to the heavy demands made upon them by their world-wide military operations, and to the world-wide shortage of transport, raw materials, and supplies for civilian consumption.

The declaration issued by the three leaders on conclusion of the conference on 1st December 1943, recorded the following military conclusions:

- The Yugoslav Partisans should be supported by supplies and equipment and also by commando operations.
- It would be desirable if Turkey should come into war on the side of the Allies before the end of the year. Noted Stalin's statement that if Turkey found herself at war with Germany, and as a result Bulgaria declared

war on Turkey or attacked her, the Soviet Union would immediately be at war with Bulgaria.

- The Conference further took note that this could be mentioned in the forthcoming negotiations to bring Turkey into the war.
- The cross-Channel invasion of France (Operation Overlord) would be launched during May 1944, in conjunction with an operation against southern France. The latter operation would be undertaken in as great strength as availability of landing craft permitted.
- The Conference also took note of Marshal Stalin's statement that the Soviet forces would launch an offensive at about the same time with the object of preventing the German forces from transferring from the Eastern to the Western Front.
- Agreed that the military staffs of the Three Powers should keep in close touch with each other in regard to the impending operations in Europe. In particular it was agreed that a cover plan to mystify and mislead the enemy as regards these operations should be concerted between the staffs concerned.

Jack and his team at Bletchley Park were given the task of fooling Hitler and his army about the exact location of the invasion through false and misleading Enigma messages. This exercise would form a significant part of 'Operation Fortitude'.

'Operation Fortitude' was the code name for the military deception employed by the Allied nations as part of an overall deception strategy (code named Bodyguard) during the build-up to the -Day landings. 'Fortitude' was divided into two sub-plans, North and South, with the aim of misleading the German high command as to the location of the imminent invasion.

Both North and South plans involved the creation of fake field armies based in Edinburgh and the south of England. The first army threatened Norway - Fortitude North; and the second Pas de Calais - Fortitude South.

Operation Fortitude was intended to divert Hitler's attention away from Normandy and, after the successful invasion on 6th June 1944, delay reinforcement by convincing the Germans that the landings were purely a diversionary attack.

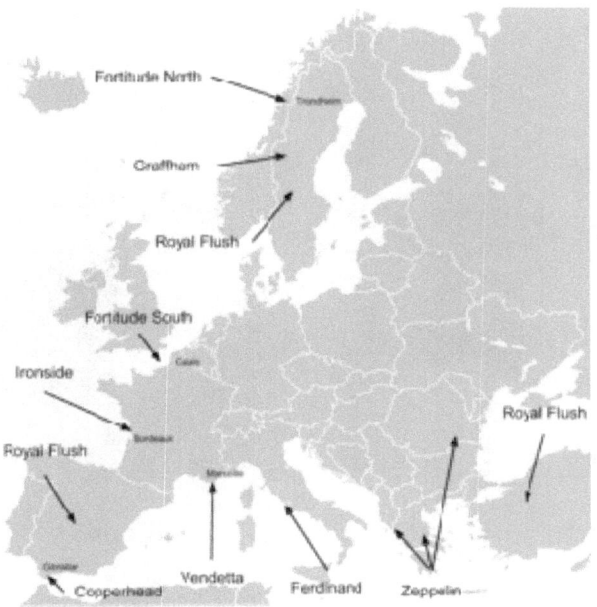

**Operation Fortitude**

It was initially envisioned that deception would occur through five main channels:

**Physical deception**: to mislead the enemy with nonexistent units through fake infrastructure and equipment, such as dummy landing craft, dummy airfields, tanks and decoy lighting.

**Controlled leaks** of information through diplomatic channels to the Germans.

**Wireless traffic**: To mislead the enemy, wireless traffic was created to simulate actual units.

**Use of German agents** controlled by the Allies through the Double Cross System to send false information to the German intelligence services.

**Public presence** of notable staff associated with phantom groups, such as FUSAG (First US Army Group), most notably the well-known US general George S. Patton.

**Placing False Tank into Position**

Operation Bodyguard and its sub-operations, including Fortitude, fooled the Nazis into spreading their defensive forces over several locations thus weakening their military strength.

Jack and his team had been successful in confusing the Germans and its allies with the cracked codes from the Enigma machine. Alan Turing and his magnificent bombe had enabled the Allies to invade mainland Europe and begin the annihilation of Hitler and the Nazis.

# 42.D-Day Has Arrived

## 6$^{th}$ June 1944

On 6$^{th}$ June 1944 the Western Allies landed in northern France, opening the long-awaited 'Second Front' against Adolf Hitler's Nazi Germany. Although they had been fighting in mainland Italy for the past nine months, the Normandy invasion was to free France and drive the Germans back to their homeland and ultimately destroy the Nazi regime.

It had been four long, tumultuous years since the invasion of France and the British retreat from Europe, three years since Hitler had attacked the Soviet Union, and two and a half since the United States had formally entered the war. By late 1942 the Germans had been stopped and forced into a slow retreat in Eastern Europe, defeated in North Africa, and challenged in Italy. American and

British bombers had rained hell on the enemy's industrial cities. Allied navies had contained the German submarine threat due to the cracking of the naval Enigma code, making possible an immense build-up of ground, sea and air power in the British Isles.

Plans for a return to France, long in preparation, were now feasible. Troops were well-trained, vast numbers of ships were accumulated, and local German forces were battered from the air. Clever deceptions had confused the enemy about just when, and especially where, the blow would fall.

Commanded by US Army General Dwight D. Eisenhower, the Normandy assault phase, code-named 'Neptune' (the entire operation was 'Overlord'), was launched when weather reports predicted satisfactory conditions on 6th June. Hundreds of amphibious ships and craft, supported by combatant warships, crossed the English Channel behind dozens of minesweepers. They arrived off the beaches before dawn. Three divisions of paratroopers (two American, one British) had already been dropped inland. Following a brief bombardment by naval guns, soldiers of six divisions (three American, two British and one Canadian) stormed ashore in five main landing areas, named 'Utah', 'Omaha', 'Gold', 'Juno' and 'Sword'. After heavy fighting a foothold was well established.

As German counterattacks were thwarted, the Allies poured men and material into France. By late July the Allied Forces were moving through France without much resistance. An additional landing in southern France in August facilitated that nation's liberation. With the Soviets advancing from the east, Hitler's armies were forcibly shoved back toward their homeland. The Second World War had entered its climactic phase.

# 43. I Do Like a Day Beside the Seaside

## But Not Omaha or Juno

Captain Peter Doherty had recently qualified from Harvard Medical School and immediately enlisted in the US Marines following a long line of Dohertys before him. After training he was assigned to the Marine Headquarters in England where he got a rare opportunity of catching up with his father, General Jack Doherty.

They arranged to meet at the Savoy and have lunch.

'Gee Dad it's great to catch up after all this time. You look great. I haven't seen you with your General's stars before. Very impressive.'

'Thanks son. Yes this war has split up many a family, some of them for good.'

'Yeah. Sad but necessary. The good guys have got to get rid of Hitler and the Nazis.'

'Don't forget the Japs.'

'Hell no! We need to beat the crap out of them. Have you heard where poor Tom is being imprisoned?'

'No, we get no information whatsoever. The Japs aren't a signatory to the Geneva Convention so they just make up the rules as they go. Under the Convention they are obligated to inform the authorities who they have imprisoned and where. Not the fucking Japs.'

'Knowing Tom, he'll survive.'

'I hope you're right, Peter. Have you got any idea where you might be assigned, son?'

'Dad, you've probably got a better idea than me. I suspect it could be retaking Europe. It's about bloody time - but I don't know.'

The two men ate their lunch and shared a bottle of French red wine.

'How's Mum coping not knowing if Tom's alive or not. It must be difficult for her with you away so much?'

'She copes, but it's not easy for her. I hope you get some time to see her while you're here.'

'Definitely! Soon as I get some leave.'

Father and son, General and Captain, shook hands and said their goodbyes.

Neither of them could know that they would not meet again until the war had ended.

Peter returned to base and waited for his orders; they didn't take long in coming.

The following day, 4th June 1944, he was ordered to report to the commander of the First Infantry Division, Major General Clarence R. Huebner.

'Captain, we are about to embark on a mission that will turn the course of the war. We are about to take back France and after that, all the territory between the French coast and Berlin.

'It's not going to be easy and we will suffer many casualties. It will be your job and the job of all the medical teams to ensure the wounded are either treated where they fall, or transported to the hospital ships for more serious medical attention. I wish you well. And don't get shot.'

'Thank you, sir. I shall try and stay in one piece. When are we due to leave?'

'Tomorrow.'

The weather was not conducive for such a massive operation and the fleet was forced to return. The next day, 6th June, the armada set sail for France heading for the Normandy coast.

# 44.D-Day

## The Longest Day

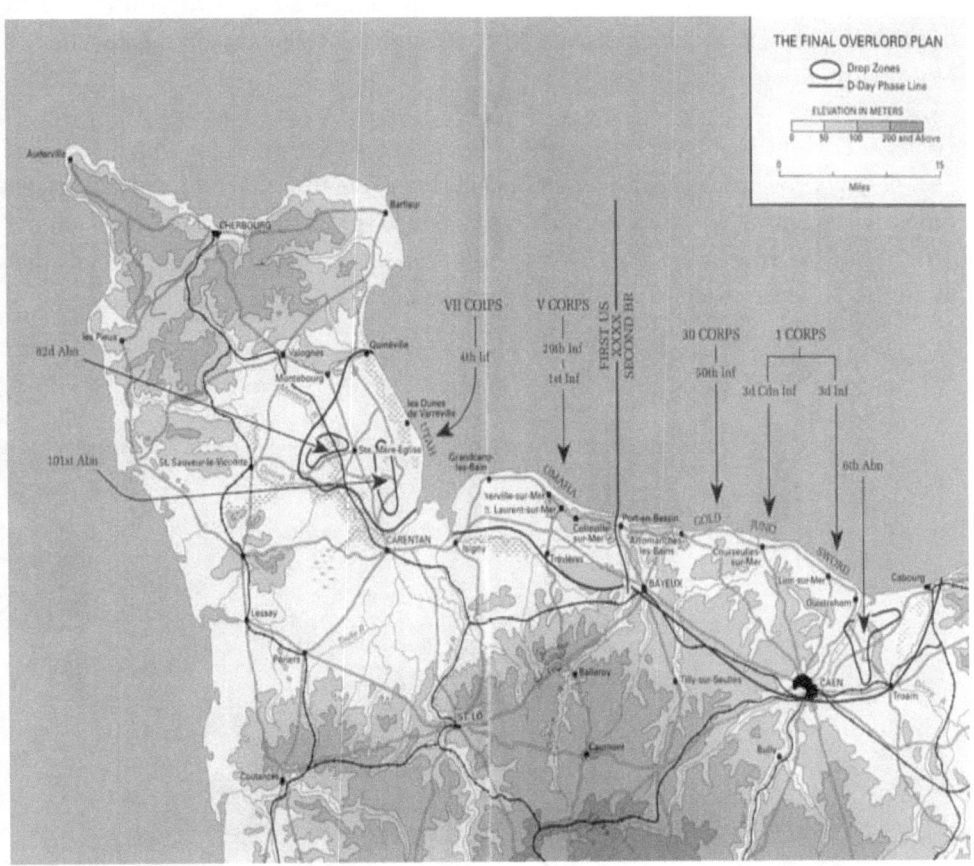

*They came, rank after relentless rank, ten lanes wide, twenty miles across, five thousand ships of every description. There were fast new attack transports, slow rust-scarred freighters, small ocean liners, Channel steamers, hospital ships, weather-beaten tankers, coasters and swarms of fussing tugs. There were endless columns of shallow-draft landing ships - great wallowing vessels, some*

*of them almost 350 feet long. ... Ahead of the convoys were processions of minesweepers, Coast Guard cutters, buoy-layers and motor launches. Barrage balloons flew above the ships. Squadrons of fighter planes weaved below the clouds. And surrounding this fantastic cavalcade of ships packed with men, guns, tanks, motor vehicles and supplies, ... was a formidable array of 702 warships.*

**The Longest Day**

One hundred and sixty thousand Allied troops landed along a fifty-mile stretch of heavily fortified French coastline to confront Nazi Germany on the beaches of Normandy, France.

General Dwight D. Eisenhower called the operation a crusade in which *'we will accept nothing less than full victory.'* More than five thousand ships and thirteen thousand aircraft supported the D-Day invasion. By day's end the Allies gained a foothold in Normandy. The D-Day toll was extremely high; more than nine thousand Allied soldiers were killed or wounded.

One hundred thousand soldiers began the march across Europe to defeat Hitler.

Omaha Beach interconnected the US and British beaches. It was a critical link between the Contentin Peninsula and the flat plain in front of Caen. Omaha was also the most restricted and heavily defended beach: for this reason the experienced US First Division was assigned to land there. The terrain was very difficult. Omaha Beach was unlike any of the other assault beaches in Normandy. Its crescent curve and unusual assortment of bluffs, cliffs and draws were immediately recognisable from the sea. It was the most defensible beach chosen for the D-Day landing. There was the strong opinion that it would be too difficult to land there and too many casualties would result. The high ground commanded all approaches to the beach from the sea and tidal flats, making the Allied troops sitting ducks for the German machine guns. To make matters worse were the narrow passages between the bluffs. Advances directly up the steep bluffs were going to be difficult in the extreme. German machine-gun nests were arranged to command all the approaches and the concrete pillboxes were sited to fire east and west, thereby exposing the Allied troops while themselves remaining concealed from bombarding warships. These pillboxes had to be taken out by direct assault. Compounding this problem was the failure of Allied intelligence to identify a nearly full-strength infantry division, the 352nd, directly behind the beach. Intelligence had them located more than twenty kilometres inland.

Captain Peter Doherty was at the back of the LCA (Landing Craft Assault) when it hit the beach, the ramp dropped and the marines waded through the water and up onto the beach.

Bullets and shells were raining down on the invading troops. Soldiers and marines were dropping everywhere and the sand was stained with the blood of the wounded and dead.

Peter started up the beach. He saw a wounded marine, crawling towards the cliff face. He crouched down beside him and asked to look at the wound. The young marine pointed to his stomach. Peter lifted his shirt and saw a small hole in the centre of his abdomen. He rolled the young man over to see his back. It was as Peter suspected - the exit wound was as big as his fist. This marine wasn't going home. Peter could do no more than reassure him and make him as comfortable as possible in the circumstances.

Doherty kept crawling up the beach, dodging bullets and shells. He couldn't believe the number of dead all over the beach. He spotted another marine, this time wounded in the leg. Peter was able to apply a bandage and called for the stretcher-bearers to take him to the LCA for transfer to the hospital ship. His knee had been shattered.

Peter was not overly religious, but seeing the mayhem around him, the dead, the dying, the wounded crying out in pain …

'This is what hell must be like,' he thought.

Doherty and his team managed to transfer twenty wounded to the hospital ship. The LCA was now on its way back for the next batch.

The young captain had been on duty for twenty-three hours, collecting the wounded and transferring them to the hospital ship for extensive treatment. He and his medical team also tended the wounded on the beach, stitching and bandaging the young frightened soldiers and sending them on their way to who knows what.

Two LCAs laden with American wounded received direct hits from the German artillery. Their second chance was obliterated in seconds.

# Omaha Beach 7th June

Captain Doherty returned to Omaha Beach the next day; there were spent shells and bullets littering the sand.

Bodies of Allied soldiers remained where they had fallen, distorted and bloodied, a grim reminder of what had transpired the day before.

Peter's orders were to follow his company inland and establish a dressing station to tend the wounded. The team were able to scale the cliffs using rope ladders and made their way inland. They found an old farmhouse which Peter decided would be adequate for the station.

Once the dressing station had been established the medical team waited for the wounded to arrive. They didn't have to wait long - a constant stream of soldiers began to materialise, most of them being carried by stretcher-bearers, others were the walking wounded.

The VII Corps advanced westwards to cut off the Cotentin Peninsula. An additional three infantry divisions had landed to reinforce the Corps. Major General J. Lawton Collins, the Corps Commander, drove his troops hard, replacing units in the front lines or sacking officers if progress was slow.

The medical teams, including Peter's, were having trouble keeping up the pace. No sooner had they established a new dressing station than they would have to pack up and move forward. The wounded were taken back to Omaha Beach to be transported to the already overcrowded hospital ships.

By day six C-46 and C-47 cargo planes were flying across the English Channel to land on improvised runways on the Normandy beachhead.

The planes ferried badly wounded men to hospitals in Great Britain. It was the job of the flight nurses to take care of the twenty-four wounded soldiers each plane could carry. Some men were missing arms or legs; others had head or chest wounds.

The Germans facing VII Corps were a mix of regiments and battle groups from several divisions, many of which had already suffered heavy casualties fighting the American airborne troops in the first days of the landings. Very few German armoured or mobile troops could be sent to this part of the front because of the threat to Caen further east. Infantry reinforcements arrived, but slowly.

By 16th June there were no further natural obstacles in front of the American forces. The German command was in some confusion. General Rommel and other commanders wished to withdraw their troops in good order into the Atlantic Wall fortifications of Cherbourg, where they could have withstood a siege for some time. Adolf Hitler, issuing orders from his headquarters in East Prussia, demanded that they hold their present lines even though this risked disaster.

Captain Doherty was transferred to the 79th Division as they had lost a significant percentage of their medical Corps in the fighting. Two days later, Peter's new battalion and a significant contingent of men and machinery from other Divisions, were on the outskirts of Cherbourg.

Major General Lawton Collins was in charge of the operation. He was confident they would be able to take Cherbourg in the next twenty-four hours. However, Lieutenant General Karl-Wilhelm von Schlieben, the German garrison commander defending the port city, thought otherwise. He had twenty-one thousand men at his disposal, however; they were either inexperienced or totally exhausted. Food, fuel and ammunition were short.

'I know that Hitler will send us reinforcements any day now. We just have to hold out until then,' Von Schlieben assured his second-in-command.

'What are our exact orders, General Von Schlieben?'

'The Führer has demanded that we fight to the death.'

Later that day, as the US troops were progressing towards the city, German planes were seen overhead. But they were not dropping much needed supplies - Hitler had ordered they drop Iron Crosses to be awarded to the brave men of Cherbourg.

'Fight to the last man. I think we'll have to,' Von Schlieben complained.

Major General Collins issued a demand to the Germans to surrender the city and save many German and US lives but General Von Schlieben refused, based on orders from Hitler.

Collins subsequently launched a general assault on 22$^{nd}$ June. Resistance was stiff at first, but the Americans slowly cleared the Germans from their bunkers and concrete pillboxes. On 26$^{th}$ June, the 79$^{th}$ Division captured Fort du Roule, which dominated the city and its defences. This finished any organised defence. Von Schlieben was captured. The harbour fortifications and the arsenal surrendered a few days later, after a token resistance. Some German troops, cut off outside the defences, held out until 1$^{st}$ July.

Captain Peter Doherty and his team marched into Cherbourg, along with twenty-five thousand other US troops.

Hitler was devastated and held Von Schlieben responsible as a very poor role model and leader.

By July the 79$^{th}$ Division had taken Lessay, crossed the Sarthe River and in early August entered Le Mans. In September they had moved east to the Franco-Belgian border frontier and crossed the Moselle River. Casualties were high and the logistics for evacuating the wounded weren't getting any easier.

The Division was given time off after such an arduous and costly few months. The Division regrouped, refreshed and readied itself to march into Germany. They moved across the Moder River in November, and through Haguenau. In December they encountered the Siegfried Line. From December until early February 1945, the Division fought many engagements around the Moder, most of them defensive until they were able to go on the offensive again.

Peter and his team were attending the wounded in the dressing station when a hail of bullets went through the station. Several of the wounded were hit as well as one of the nurses. Peter received a wound to the right leg just above the knee and another in his hip. His medical comrades attended him and a transport aircraft was summoned to take him and the other wounded back to England to be treated.

This would be the end of Peter's war.

He was flown home to the United States in May 1945.

# 45. The Colour Purple

## Japan's Enigma Machine

Baron Hiroshi Oshima, a Japanese General and Ambassador to Nazi Germany prior to the Second World War, was able to purchase an Enigma Machine with the approval of Hitler. The objective was for Japan to replicate and possibly improve the German encryption device. The Japanese soon created a similar machine, which the Americans, on learning of its existence, code-named 'Red'.

This was the machine the Japanese Navy used from 1931 to 1936 when the American code-breakers cracked it.

Having learnt of the security breach the Japanese went about creating a new system based on a 97 Alphabetical Typewriter. This device was better known by its US code-name, 'Purple'.

The Purple Machine comprised two typewriters as well as an electrical rotor system with a twenty-five character alphabetic switchboard. Similar to the Enigma Machine, the first typewriter was the method by which the plain text, or unencrypted message, could be manually typed. The typewriter was built to be compatible with English, and Roman, adding a level of mystery through language choice.

The major difference between the Enigma Machine, which presented the text in the form of blinking lights, and the Purple Machine was that Purple used a second electric typewriter, which would type the cypher text, or encrypted message, onto a piece of paper. This was a major improvement on the Enigma Machine.

The Purple Machine in addition to its encryption capabilities also used a secret key that was changed on a daily basis. This meant that even if a Purple Machine were stolen, it would be useless without the key of the day.

Additionally, as the key changed every day, code-breakers would not be able to find patterns in messages sent over several days. The daily key would be inputted into the device by the arrangement of the switchboard and rotors. The switchboard contained twenty-five connections, which could be arranged in six pairs of connections, yielding over 70,000,000,000,000 possible arrangements, which would determine the method of encryption. This would make Purple extremely difficult to crack. Add to that the daily key.

Eventually, Lt Francis A. Raven, a member of the team, discovered a pattern being used by the Japanese in their daily keys. He noticed that each month was broken into three ten-day segments in which a pattern was discerned. The Purple cypher was effectively broken and Japanese secrets were exposed.

The cracking of the Purple Machine's code remained a closely kept secret - not even the British or its allies were aware of the American breakthrough. They were able to track Japanese naval troop movement as well as other military communications.

Therefore why didn't the US know of the Japanese plan to attack Pearl Harbour? Or did they?

# 46.Like Father Like Son, Again

Tom and Pete Doherty would visit their parents for six weeks each year while they were stationed in Germany and London. When the war broke out it was decided that the trip was too dangerous.

Tom had followed his father's and grandfather's footsteps and enrolled in the Academy graduating as an officer in the Marines. Peter, on the other hand enrolled at Harvard to study medicine.

Tom had been assigned to the 3$^{rd}$ Defence Battalion at Pearl Harbour. He was delighted that his first posting was in such a beautiful location as Hawaii.

That was until 7$^{th}$ December 1941.

Tom was the Ford Island duty officer and watched Privates First Class Frank Dudovick, James D. Young, and Private Paul O. Zeller USMCR the Marine colour guard, march up and take their posts for Colours. Satisfied that all looked in order outside, Tom stepped back into his office to check if the assistant officer-of-the-day, Gerry Hudson, was ready to play the recording for sounding Colours on the loudspeaker. The sound of two heavy explosions however, sent the Marine officer running to the door. He reached it just in time to see a Japanese bomber fly past number 1010 Dock and release a torpedo. The torpedo struck the battleship *California*.

Hudson and Tom looked on in awe as wave after wave of Japanese planes strafed the harbour below them. Zeros and BSN torpedo-bombers were swarming over the harbour dropping their lethal cargo. US ships were exploding and sinking quickly, their crews unable to escape the burning wreckage. So absorbed were they in the attack below, Tom and Gerry did not notice the two Zeros approaching from behind until it was too late. The Japanese fighter started firing; Gerry was riddled with Japanese bullets and died instantly. Tom received a leg wound and dropped to the ground, pretending to be dead. The Zeros passed over again very low - they were satisfied the two Navy officers had been eliminated. Tom squinted through one eye at the planes as they passed over. He could see the two pilots and the Rising Sun; there was no doubt who the enemy was.

The Japanese attack lasted two hours and created absolute havoc.

**Japanese Bombing at Pearl Harbour**

# American Losses:

4 battleships sunk

3 battleships damaged

1 battleship grounded

2 other ships sunk

3 cruisers damaged

3 destroyers damaged

3 other ships damaged

188 aircraft destroyed

159 aircraft damaged

2,402 killed

1,247 wounded

## Japanese Losses

4 midget submarines sunk

1 midget submarine grounded

29 aircraft destroyed

64 killed

1 captured

Ensign Kazuo Sakamaki became America's first prisoner of war in WWII when his midget submarine ran aground after his attempted attack at Pearl Harbour on 7th December 1941. Although initially wanting to commit suicide in shame for being captured, he gradually developed a more positive outlook, and spent the entire war in various POW camps in Wisconsin, Tennessee, Louisiana, and

Texas. After the war's end, Sakamaki returned to his home in Japan, soon married, and started a job in the Nagoya area at Toyota Motor Corporation.

Tom lay where he dropped until being discovered by a group of Marines looking for casualties.

They stretchered him down on a Jeep to the dock and transferred him to the Navy hospital ship the USS *Solace*.

**USS *Solace***

The doctor examined the gun shot wounds and found three bullets had entered his left leg and another two in his right. Tom had been fortunate in that only one bullet had lodged in the leg. The others had passed right through leaving a hole that could be cleaned and stitched.

Nevertheless the one remaining bullet would require surgery to remove it.

Tom was operated on the next day and was transferred to the Navy hospital at Pearl Harbour.

**Navy Hospital**

He recuperated for about three weeks reporting back for duty with a full medical clearance. He was itching to have a go at the Japanese

Two days after Pearl Harbour they attacked the Philippines. On Saturday 14th February the American defensive lines finally broke. General Macarthur and his battle-weary troops withdrew declaring they would return.

By this time, the Japanese had captured Borneo, Celebes and Sarawak.

How was the United States going to halt the Japanese juggernaut?

# 15th February 1942

Singapore fell to the might of the Japanese assault resulting in the capture of some one hundred thousand Allied prisoners against the cost of two thousand Japanese soldiers.

Winston Churchill declared the fall to be the 'largest capitulation in British history'.

# 47. Singapore Falls

## Let the Terror Begin

Britain prided itself on its naval strength in Singapore. A fleet of warships was stationed there, led by the pride of the fleet, *Prince of Wales* and the battle cruiser *Repulse*.

On 8$^{th}$ December 1941, both ships put out to sea and headed north up the Malay coast to where the Japanese were landing. On 10$^{th}$ December, an infamous day in British naval history, both ships were sunk by repeated attacks from Japanese torpedo bombers. The RAF had already been effectively destroyed and could therefore offer no protection. The loss of both warships had a devastating impact on morale in Britain. Sir Winston Churchill wrote in his memoirs:

'I put the telephone down. I was thankful to be alone. In all the war I never received a more direct shock.'

If Singapore was to be saved, only the Army was in a position to halt the Japanese advance.

Lieutenant General Arthur Percival had ninety thousand men under his command including British, Indian and Australian troops. The Japanese advanced with sixty-five thousand men led by General Tomoyuki Yamashita. The majority of the Japanese troops had fought in the Manchurian/Chinese campaign and were battle-hardened. Most of Percival's men had never seen combat.

The first confrontation took place at Jitra in Malaya between 11$^{th}$ and 12$^{th}$ December 1941.

Percival's forces were routed and withdrew in full retreat. The Japanese attack was based on speed, ferocity and surprise. To accelerate their advance, the Japanese used bicycles as well as the more traditional forms of transport. The

Japanese *modus operandi* was demonstrated when captured wounded Allied soldiers were killed where they lay. Those who were not injured but had surrendered were also murdered. Some captured Australian troops were doused with petrol and burned to death. Locals who had helped the Allies were tortured before being murdered.

The brutality of the Japanese soldiers shocked the British. But the effectiveness of the Japanese war machine was demonstrated when they captured the capital of Malaya, Kuala Lumpur, on 11th January 1942.

All the indications were that the Japanese would attack Singapore across the Johor Strait. General Wavell, the British commander in the region, was ordered by Churchill to fight and never surrender Singapore.

On 31st January 1942, the British and Australian forces withdrew across the causeway that separated Singapore from Malaya. It was clear that this would be their final stand. Percival spread his men across a seventy-mile line, the entire coastline of the island.

It became obvious that Percival had spread his defences far too thinly. This was to be a fatal miscalculation on his part.

On 8th February 1942, the Japanese attacked across the Johor Strait as had been predicted. Because Percival had spread his defences so thinly the Allied soldiers were too far away to try and halt the deadly advance. On 8th February, twenty-three thousand Japanese soldiers attacked Singapore. They advanced with speed and ferocity.

Harry and Julie were summoned by the Governor to Government house to receive a briefing.

> 'Well, I am sure you are aware the Japanese hordes are at our doorstep. I think it is essential that we point out in no uncertain terms that our hospital is out of bounds, as it were,' Sir Shenton came straight to the point.

> 'Certainly, Sir Shenton. I can't imagine any invading army bringing harm to hospital patients and the staff who are caring for them. Besides, it's prohibited by the Geneva Convention.'

> 'Harry, I'm not sure that the Japanese are a signatory to the Convention.'

'Sir, may I make a suggestion? Julie can stay here in Government House while I return to Alexandria to make sure the hospital has the appropriate Red Cross flags etc. flying. So there is no mistaking the hospital is protected ground.'

'No, Harry I'll come with you. I owe it to my patients.'

'No, Julie, Harry is right. You should stay here. For the time being anyway.'

Julie reluctantly agreed and Harry made his way to Alexandria Hospital.

Harry arrived at the hospital at 12.30 pm and checked the Red Cross flags and banners; they could be clearly seen from all sides. He conducted a round of the wards reassuring all the patients that all was well.

Harry observed the first Japanese troops from the hospital's upstairs verandah around 1:00 pm. They advanced in single file, led by a soldier carrying the red and white Japanese flag. All were dressed in green uniforms, steel helmets, camouflaged with tree branches and twigs, and armed with rifles with bayonets and submachine guns. They were moving up from the Ayer Rajah Road, with another group advancing towards the Sisters' Quarters. Harry asked Captain Bartlett to greet the soldiers and although the hospital was clearly marked with red crosses, the international symbol for medical sanctuary, Harry decided to take no chances. The first Japanese soldier entered the hospital compound; Captain Bartlett went out to meet him. The Captain raised his arms to signal his peaceful intent and pointed at the red crosses on the hospital. As he spoke the word 'Hospital,' the soldier raised his rifle and fired at the Captain at point-blank range.

Japanese soldiers began to enter the hospital murdering the patients they found there.

Harry and the Commanding Officer Lieutenant Colonel Craven discussed whether they should formally surrender. It was decided that one more effort to show they were a medical facility was called for.

Lieutenant Craven grabbed a Red Cross flag and held it at the window. The Japanese responded with a shot, which missed Lieutenant Craven, striking the wall behind him.

The hospital became a war zone with guns firing inside and out, screams could be heard between explosions and gunfire. Patients and medical staff were running for cover everywhere. Harry made his way down to the ground floor about thirty minutes after the assault began; Lieutenant Colonel Craven was with him.

What they discovered was horrific, some fifty dead and many more wounded; the floor awash with blood and grey matter.

The two men made their way to the operating theatre.

Apparently, a Japanese soldier had entered the room and found the surgical team standing together in the middle of the floor with their hands above their heads. He motioned the men into the corridor. There, a dozen Japanese soldiers set upon them with bayonets. Dr Rogers was stabbed in the right side of the chest and two more times as he lay on the ground. Dr Parkinson, who tried to run around the corner into the main corridor, was gunned down. Two more were killed by bayonet. The patient in the theatre, who was under anaesthetic, was bayoneted to death on the operating table.

Captain Smiley, Chief Surgeon, received a thrust to the breast, which was deflected away from his heart by a cigarette case in his pocket. He blocked the next thrust with his arm and took the dagger in his groin. The next two thrusts severely injured his right arm and hand. Captain Smiley fell onto Private Sutton, who had thus far escaped attack. The Captain told Sutton to fall down with him and pretend to be dead. After the soldiers left, Harry and Craven found their colleagues. They dressed Smiley's wounds as best they could. Both Smiley and Sutton lived to tell the tale.

In another section of the hospital, the Japanese were busy assembling a group of more than two hundred surrendered men comprising hospital staff and the walking wounded, some of them in splints and bandages and hobbling on casts. Their hands were tied behind their backs and then the men were tied into groups of eight. These groups were led out of the hospital by the north wing. A group of about sixty officers and men gathered from the second floor, including Harry, joined the larger group.

The prisoners were herded along the railway track through a drain tunnel under the railway embankment to Ayer Rajah Road and then to a row of buildings a quarter of a mile from the hospital and set about fifty yards back from the road. Men who were too weak to walk were allowed to lay their arms on the shoulders of more able-bodied men. But those who fell were bayoneted and left for dead.

As fighting around the hospital was still intense, the prisoners were also subjected to the shelling of their own army.

The prisoners were packed into three small rooms, the biggest of which measured approximately ten feet by twelve feet. Each room was crammed with fifty to seventy men. The doors were barricaded with lengths of wood and the windows shuttered and nailed up. There was no ventilation - the temperature outside was thirty-five degrees with eighty percent humidity. The men remained tied together, but managed to take turns sitting on the floor to rest. A number of men found it possible to untie themselves but there seemed no way out of the building short of a rescue. The men were forced to relieve themselves where they stood. All were thirsty, many severely dehydrated. Some became delirious and slipped into unconsciousness. A number did not survive to see morning.

The following morning, a Japanese officer opened the door of one room and said in broken English,

'We are taking you behind the lines. You will get water on the way.'

When the Japanese began taking the men out two-by-two along the courtyard and around the latrine, the prisoners were encouraged. More than one hundred men were led on the so-called 'water march'.

Soon the remaining prisoners began to hear screams of anguish, and cries of 'Oh my God,' 'Mother,' 'Don't, don't.' The sight of a Japanese soldier wiping the blood off his bayonet confirmed their worst fears: the prisoners were being systematically massacred.

Suddenly, the sound of shelling could be heard. One shell struck the end of a building and tore the doors and window shutters, filling the air with dust. A number of men sprinted from the building. The majority of these men were shot down, but a few of them managed to get clear of the buildings and into the brush surrounding the storm drain. One of them was Harry, along with Corporal C.N.C. Bryer, Privates S.W.J Hoskins and F.A.H. Gurd, Captain R. de Warrenne Waller and Medical Corporal G.W. Johnson. These were the only men out of two hundred and fifty taken who lived to tell their stories.

While the massacre was underway across the railway tracks on 15th February, the hospital had become a battle station. The Japanese allowed no medical activity. Later in the day, the remaining prisoners cleaned up the wards. Medical Ward 6 was turned into a mortuary.

At 8:00 pm on 15$^{th}$ February the Allies surrendered to the Japanese.

Harry and the other escapees made their way back to central Singapore knowing there was no way to get off the island. They figured it would be best to join the British and Australian troops and the civilian population - at least they stood a chance as POWs.

The Japanese took one hundred thousand men and women prisoner in Singapore. Many had just arrived and had not fired a shot in anger. Nine thousand of these men died building the Burma-Thailand railway. The people of Singapore fared worse. Many were of Chinese origin - over fifty thousand of them - and they were slaughtered by the Japanese.

The fall of Singapore was a humiliation for the British government. The Japanese had been portrayed as useless soldiers only capable of fighting the militarily inferior Chinese. How wrong they were.

The commander of the Australian forces in Singapore, Major General Gordon Bennet said before escaping the carnage,

> 'The whole operation seems incredible: 550 miles in 55 days – forced back by a small Japanese army of only two divisions, riding stolen bicycles and without artillery support.'

Leaving the twenty-two thousand Diggers behind to deal with their fate, Bennet escaped the island on the basis of being more useful to the cause back home in Australia.

> *Gordon Bennet escaped two hours after the surrender of Singapore. His aide, Captain Gordon Walker swam out from the waterfront to a sampan, rowed it ashore and with several other officers started down the strait. They got aboard a junk crowded with British officers and loaded with anti-aircraft shells, slipped past the silent guns of Blakang Mati and so southward for five days. Walker said. 'All of us were in a bad state of nerves and everyone wanted to run the boat. It was hell. After twenty four hours we began to eat and took a cup of water a day, a handful of rice and some carefully divided cubes of pineapple and bully beef.'*

*From the junk the Bennet party transferred to the* Tern, *a thirty-foot police launch formerly in the Singapore harbour service, and went through Sumatra by way of Jambi, Muaratebo and Padang to Java and safety.*

Singapore is Silent *by George Weller*

Hell on earth was about to begin.

**Major General Gordon Bennet**

# 48.Japanese Hospitality

**A Section of Changi Prison**

Changi was one of the more notorious Japanese prisoner of war camps. Changi was used to imprison Malayan civilians and Allied soldiers. The treatment of POWs at Changi was harsh but fitted in with the belief held by the Japanese Imperial Army that those who had surrendered to it were guilty of dishonouring their country and family and as such deserved to be treated in no other way.

For this reason, forty thousand men from the surrender of Singapore were marched to the northern tip of the island where they were imprisoned at a military base called Selerang, near the village of Changi. The British civilian population of Singapore was imprisoned in Changi Prison itself, one mile away from Selerang. Eventually, any reference to the area was simply made to 'Changi'.

For the first few months the POWs at Changi were allowed to do as they wished with little interference from the Japanese. There was just enough food and medicine provided and to begin with the Japanese seemed indifferent to what the POWs did. Concerts were organised, as were quizzes and sporting events. The camp was organised by the officers into battalions and regiments and strong military discipline was maintained. However, by Easter 1942, the attitude of the Japanese had changed. They organised work parties to repair the damaged docks in Singapore and food and medicine became scarce. More significantly, the Japanese made it clear that they had not signed the Geneva Convention and that they ran the camp based on their own rules.

As 1942 moved on, deaths from dysentery and vitamin deficiencies increased dramatically.

Four Allied POWs - two Australians and two British - attempted to escape, enraging the Japanese administration, who demanded that everyone in the camp sign a document declaring that they would not attempt to escape. This was universally refused. As a result, twenty thousand POWs were herded into the Selerang Barracks Square and told that they would remain there until the order was given to sign the document.

The Selerang Barracks, originally built to accommodate eight hundred men, consisted of a parade ground surrounded on three sides by three-storey buildings. A number of smaller houses for officers and married couples were spread out in the spacious grounds. Nearly twenty thousand men crammed into a parade ground of about one hundred and twenty-eight by two hundred and ten metres.

**Selerang Barracks Square**

An Australian POW, George Aspinall documented the situation:

> *The first and most urgent problem we had to face up to was the lack of toilet facilities. Each barracks building had about four to six toilets, which were flushed from small cisterns on the roofs. But the Japanese cut the water off, and these toilets couldn't be used. The Japanese only allowed one water tap to be used, and people used to line up in the early hours of the morning and that queue would go on all day. You were allowed one water bottle of water per man per day, just one quart for your drinking, washing, and everything else. Not that there was much washing done under the circumstances.'*

Dr Harry de Neville was becoming very concerned with the health of the troops and he, along with Lieutenant Colonel 'Weary' Dunlop, knew that if this stand-off lasted much longer men were going to die.

'We need to get access to more clean water Lieutenant Colonel. If we don't, they'll start dropping like flies.'

'I know Harry. By the way, call me 'Weary'. Everyone else does.'

'Why do they call you Weary?'

'It's my surname - Dunlop. Tyres. Weary.'

'Oh, I get it. Anyway - do you think we could approach the Japanese? See if we can increase the water ration?'

'Harry, we can try. But I think these bastards are going to refuse. Until the assurance of non-escape is signed they're going to squeeze tighter and tighter.'

'Do you reckon we all should sign it and end this fucking stalemate?'

'I do. It's not worth the rice paper it's written on.'

Harry and Weary made a heartfelt plea to the Japanese commander.

'Sir, we beg you to increase the food and water ration to our men. It's causing dysentery and other illnesses. These could spread throughout the entire group.'

'I will increase the ration as soon as your stubborn men sign the document. We have politely asked them to sign. Not before.'

Harry and Weary retreated to the barracks knowing that more and more prisoners would die each day they were detained in the unholy square.

After three very hot and humid days and despite the oppressive conditions, the POWs still refused to back down.

General Fukuye ordered the commander of the British and Australian troops in Changi, Lt-Gen E. B. Holmes, and his deputy, Lieutenant Colonel Frederick Galleghan, to attend the execution of the four recent escapees: Breavington, Gale, Waters and Fletcher. One of the Australians, Breavington, pleaded to no avail that he was solely responsible for the escape attempt and should be the only one executed. The Indian National Army guards carried out their executions with rifles on $2^{nd}$ September. The initial volley was non-fatal, and the wounded men had to plead to be finished off.

This action had no effect on the POWs' position. The Japanese pulled out ten men and marched them to the local beach and shot them all. Despite this, still no-one signed the document.

Only when the men were threatened with an epidemic by moving the hospital into the square was the order given that the document should be signed.

Harry and Weary had made it very clear to the officers that moving the sick into the barracks would not only finish off their patients, it would spread disease throughout the ranks – they were already at the end of their tether.

However, having agreed, the commanding officer made it clear that the document was non-binding, as it had been signed under duress. He also knew that his men desperately needed the medicine that the Japanese would have withheld if the document had not been signed. But this episode marked a point of no return for the POWs at Changi.

Harry and Julie had not seen each other since Julie farewelled Harry at Government House that terrible day when the Japanese marched into Singapore. She assumed he was alive although she had heard of the rumours of a massacre at Alexandria Hospital where they both worked. She knew Harry - he would have managed to live.

Being a doctor, Julie was kept busy with looking after the three thousand-odd civilian prisoners at the second Changi Prison, quite close to where Harry was being held.

The civilians were slightly better off than the POWs, with better food rations and water but very little medicine. This made Julie's job all the more difficult.

As in the men's prison, dysentery and malaria were the greatest killers.

Little Lara was feeling the effects also. Julie had difficulty in finding the right food for her natural development. Milk was virtually non-existent; the closest Julie could acquire was coconut milk.

She was near the perimeter fence hoping to get a glimpse of Harry, something she did regularly but without success. This day, she saw two men with a Japanese escort striding over the parade ground heading for the commander's office. She swore it was Harry but couldn't be sure - the man was terribly skinny and wore a hat. She dare not yell out, as she would be beaten severely for unruly behaviour. She waited until the two men returned to the male prison. This time she was sure it was Harry, her darling Harry. She now knew for certain that her beloved husband was alive.

The Japanese used the POWs at Changi for slave labour. The formula was very simple; if you worked, you would get fed. If you didn't work, you would starve. Men were made to work in the docks where they loaded munitions onto ships. They were also used to clear sewers damaged in the attack on Singapore. The men who were too ill to work relied on those who could work for their food. Sharing what were already meagre supplies became a way of life – true mateship.

The number of POWs kept at Changi dropped quite markedly as men were constantly shipped out to other areas in the Japanese Empire to work. Men were sent to Borneo or Thailand to work on the Burma-Thai railway or to Japan itself where they were made to work in the mines. More captured soldiers, airmen and sailors from a variety of Allied nations replaced them. Malaria, dysentery and dermatitis were common, as were beatings for not working hard enough.

In 1943, the seven thousand men left at Selerang were moved to the prison in Changi. It was built to hold one thousand. The Japanese crammed five or six men in a cell designed for one. With such overcrowding, disease was rife and spread throughout the prison. The majority of the Red Cross parcels were never distributed; therefore the men at Changi had to rely on their own wits to survive. An example of POW ingenuity was that the army medics made tablets convincing the Japanese guards they were a cure for VD. The tablets became a best seller and they could then buy genuine medicine for their own men in an attempt to aid those who were sick.

As the end of the Pacific War approached, rations to the POWs were reduced and the work requirement increased. POWs were forced to dig tunnels and foxholes in the hills around Singapore, affording the Japanese places to hide and fight when the Allies finally reached Singapore.

Many POWs believed that the Japanese would kill them as the Allies got near to Singapore. This never happened. When Emperor Hirohito told the people of Japan that the war 'has gone not necessarily to our advantage', the Japanese soldiers at Changi simply handed over their weapons and became prisoners themselves.

By the time Changi was liberated over eight thousand Australian POWs had died. The British lost over twelve thousand.

**Accommodation at Changi**

# 49. We Will Fight Them on the Beaches

## And in the Jungle

Tom was promoted to Captain and assigned to the *Saratoga*, a Lexington-class aircraft carrier built for the United States Navy during the 1920s. Originally designed as a battle cruiser, she was converted into one of the Navy's first aircraft carriers during construction to comply with the Washington Naval Treaty of 1922. The ship entered service in 1928 and was assigned to the Pacific Fleet for her entire career. *Saratoga* and her sister ship, *Lexington*, were used to develop and refine carrier tactics in a series of annual exercises before World War II. On more than one occasion these included successful surprise attacks on Pearl Harbour, Hawaii - ironic! She was one of three pre-war US fleet aircraft carriers, along with *Enterprise* and *Ranger*, to serve throughout World War II.

Tom's first major engagement was Guadalcanal.

Japanese troops arrived on Guadalcanal on 8th June 1942, to construct an air base. Strategically, to possess an air base was important if Japan was to control the lines of communication between the United States and Australia. American marines landed two months later, and included in that contingent was Captain Tom Doherty. Their objective was to capture the airfield hence protecting the important sea-lanes. Up until then, few people outside the South Pacific had ever heard of that two thousand five hundred square-mile speck of jungle in the Solomon Islands. The following six months would ensure Guadalcanal was as well known as Pearl Harbour and would prove to be the turning point in the Pacific war.

Operationally, the Battle of Guadalcanal was notable for the interrelationship of a complex series of engagements on the ground, at sea, and in the air. Tactically, what stood out was the resolve and resourcefulness of the US Marines, supported by Australian and New Zealand troops whose tenacious defence of the air base dubbed 'Henderson Field' enabled the Americans to secure air superiority.

By the end of the battle on 9th February 1943, the Japanese had lost two-thirds of the thirty-one thousand army troops committed to the island, whereas the US and its allies had lost less than seven thousand soldiers of the sixty thousand deployed. The ship losses on both sides were heavy. The US lost twenty-eight while the Japanese Navy lost thirty-eight. But by far the most significant loss for the Japanese was the decimation of their elite group of naval aviators. Japan, after Guadalcanal, no longer had a realistic hope of withstanding the counter offensive of an increasingly powerful Allied force.

Tom Doherty was watching the men in his company board the amphibious landing craft (LVCP). The last craft, number seven had one space left: it was his.

The landing force split into two groups, with one group assaulting Guadalcanal, and the other, including Tom's D Company, attacking Tulagi and nearby islands. Allied warships bombarded the invasion beaches while US carrier aircraft bombed Japanese positions on the target islands and destroyed fifteen Japanese seaplanes at their base near Tulagi.

Three thousand US Marines assaulted Tulagi and two nearby small islands, Gavutu and Tanambogo. The Japanese defending the naval and seaplane bases on the three islands fiercely resisted the Marine attacks. Tom's D Company fought ferociously, supported by the other Marines and they eventually secured all three islands Tulagi on 8th August, and Gavutu and Tanambogo by 9th August. The Japanese defenders were killed almost to the last man, while the Marines suffered one hundred and twenty-two killed, ten from D Company.

**Japanese Dead on Talagi Beach**

Tom ordered his troops to surround Henderson Field to ward off any Japanese Attacks. He knew the Japanese strength had been much depleted but he also knew they were likely to bring in fresh troops with the objective to retake the airfield.

He was right. It was quickly reinforced with elements of the Japanese 17th Army in the form of a brigade of eleven hundred men under Colonel Kiyono Ichiki, whose forces had originally been designated for the assault on Midway two months earlier.

**Captain Ichiki**

Tom was walking the perimeter of the airbase at about 11 pm checking the defences and ensuring his men were alert and ready for an attack. A sergeant approached him accompanied by an islander, Jacob Vouza. Jacob had been employed as a scout. Tom could not help notice that Vouza had been badly wounded and should receive medical attention but Jacob insisted on speaking to Tom first. Vouza's ability as a scout had already been proven when the US 1$^{st}$ Marine Division landed on Guadalcanal on 7$^{th}$ August 1942. That same day, Vouza rescued an aviator from USS *Wasp* who was shot down in Japanese-held territory. He guided the pilot to American lines where he met the Marines for the first time.

On 20$^{th}$ August, while scouting for suspected Japanese outposts, soldiers of the Ichiki detachment, a battalion-strength force of the Japanese 28$^{th}$ Infantry Regiment, captured Vouza. Having found a small American flag in Vouza's loincloth, the Japanese tied him to a tree and tortured him for information about Allied forces. Vouza was questioned for hours, but refused to talk. He was then bayoneted in both of his arms, throat, shoulder, face, and stomach, and left to die.

After his captors departed, he freed himself by chewing through the ropes and made his way through the miles of jungle to American lines.

> 'Boss, I must warn you. There's many Japs. Maybe two hundred and fifty, maybe five hundred. Coming to attack you any minute.'

> 'How do you know this Jacob?'

Jacob explained to Tom what had happened to him and how he had heard the Japanese soldiers talking amongst themselves about their plans. They certainly didn't reckon on Jacob living and divulging their plans to the Americans.

**Jacob Vouza**

Tom quickly alerted his men of the imminent attack.

> 'OK fellas! All hell is about to break loose. Any rumours you may have heard about the Japs being invincible is crap. They bleed just like the rest of us. They're shit-scared when they feel the cold hard steel of a bayonet.

> 'You know the old British order 'don't shoot until you see the whites of their eyes'? Bullshit! Start firing as soon as you hear any fucking noise in the jungle! And don't stop shooting until they stop returning fire. We've got the big guns to back us up so chances are they'll kill most of the little bastards before we even have to fire a shot. Good luck boys, do your best.'

Tom ran back to his command position at the airfield. The first shots were heard at midnight; the last were at 5 pm. The Japanese commander, Colonel Kiyonao Ichiki, had underestimated the strength of the allied forces opposing him.

Ichiki's assault was defeated with heavy Japanese losses in what became known as the 'Battle of the Tenaru'. When day broke, Captain Tom Doherty's company along with the other US companies counterattacked Ichiki's surviving troops, killing many more of them. The dead included Ichiki himself, though it has been claimed that he committed *seppuku* after realising the magnitude of his defeat, rather than dying in combat. In total, all but one hundred and twenty-eight of the original nine hundred and seventeen members of the Ichiki Regiment's First Element were killed in the battle.

The Marines suffered thirty-four killed and about eighty wounded. Ten marines were captured - unfortunately one of the ten was Tom. He had entered the jungle fringe when he heard a noise after the battle had ceased; it was a well-armed Japanese soldier; a captain like him.

His Japanese captor disarmed him and proceeded to march him deeper into the jungle until they reached a small group of soldiers. They all jumped up and started to prod him with their bayonets but the Captain ordered them to stop and instructed two soldiers to tie Tom to a tree. There was Tom, bound to a large tree while his captors were discussing what to do with him. Despite only knowing a few Japanese words he got the gist of the conversation.

They were divided between the 'let's torture the bastard, learn what he knows and then kill him' as opposed to 'let's take him back and keep him as a POW'.

Finally Captain Ichino decided they would take Tom back to what was left of their camp and transport him over to a POW camp in Singapore.

Tom was loaded onto a merchant ship along with the other nine prisoners. They were placed in a cargo hold for the five-day journey to their new home. They were given very little food, mainly rice and inadequate amounts of water. The temperature in the airless cavern was estimated to be forty degrees and the humidity level was ninety per cent, an almost deadly environment.

When the ship berthed at Singapore dock and the covers were removed from the hold the nine prisoners could hardly move. The Japanese guards encouraged them with bayonets and whips. Tom and his shipmates were thrown onto the back of an army truck and taken over very rough roads to a POW camp called the River Valley Road Camp. It was right in the heart of Singapore and detained mainly Australians with some American POWs.

The routine for Tom and the other prisoners was harsh; the guards would often whip them for the slightest indiscretion and on occasion they were forced to witness a beheading.

# January 1945

Tom and about nine hundred prisoners from the United States and Australia mainly, were herded into the parade ground and then marched through the streets of Singapore and down to the docks. There waiting for them were a number of rusting old cargo ships.

'The guards using bamboo sticks forced us all into the hold. Cattle were treated better. I had experienced a similar hellhole before but not with so many men.'

# 50. Hell Ships

## Tom Doherty's Account

The Japanese guards made it clear they wanted around four hundred and fifty of us in each hold.

The poor bastards below were shouting and pleading for them not to let any more men in. But the louder they shouted the more intense the guards became pushing us down into the depths of hell.

I had suffered under the Japanese since my capture but nothing had prepared me for this. The only slightly amusing thing was the name of the ship: *Fuku Maru*.

In the hold there was standing room only for us poor wretches, all of us packed in like sardines, with no toilet facilities. Most had dysentery, malaria and beriberi, a disease caused by our limited diet and marked by pain and paralysis.

The guards battened down the hatches, the rank, humid, black dungeon creating a claustrophobic terror amongst the men. These horrible ships were unknown to us but would eventually be known as 'hell ships' and with good reason. Some of the most macabre episodes of the war occurred on these ships- men driven crazy by thirst killed fellow prisoners to drink their blood.

Submarines and aircraft sank nineteen of the fifty-six hell ships; many of the allied prisoners were killed in these attacks by their own side. Twenty-two thousand POWs died en route to camps in Japan and Taiwan.

Down in the bowels of the *Fuku Maru* the heat was unbelievable. Temperatures quickly reached in excess of 45C.

I could not move. No one could. You couldn't sit or lie down. And the smell was indescribable; an overpowering stench of excrement, urine, vomit, sweat, weeping ulcers and rotting flesh clogged the atmosphere.

Thirst became our biggest problem. At no time were we given water, none whatsoever. You start to hallucinate and see mirages, and that is the most dangerous thing. People died down in the holds from suffocation or heart attacks. Their bodies lay among us.

Six days out of Singapore, I wondered how much more I could take. Then, I felt a tremendous blast - a torpedo tore through the hold. The ship shuddered and listed. We were going down.

A pack of US submarines had attacked the convoy not knowing the nature of the pitiful human cargo.

The water was lapping the hatches and by some miracle I was washed out. The sea was a mass of thick oil emanating from the twelve Japanese hell ships that had been sunk by the attack. Those of us who could swim were the only ones who survived.

I put my head down and swam like I had never swum before gulping oil the whole time, surrounded by debris and flames. I thought I would never make it. But I did.

When I was a safe distance from the sinking ship I stopped swimming and trod water for a while. The scene was one of sinking ships, fire on the water and bodies floating everywhere.

Two hundred and forty-four of my comrades on the *Fuku Maru* died that night. They had survived the camps and the horrendous work details, the starvation and the conditions in the holds of the hell ships only to be killed by 'friendly fire'.

I had been able to grab a single-man life raft as it came floating past. Exhausted, I hauled myself into it.

As night descended so did the temperature. It became bitterly cold but I knew the only way to survive was to stay awake. With the sunrise, I could see what surrounded me - water, nothing else, just an endless horizon of water. I could barely see due to the unrelenting glare reflecting off the water. The sunburn was becoming intense and I developed salt-water immersion sores which were made even more painful when crude oil got into the fissures. I wondered if I would have been better off dying like my comrades.

As the sun set and it became night it became bitterly cold once more.

By the time the sun rose on the fifth day, I could no longer see. I had no eyebrows or hair on my head. I think the sheer shock of what was happening to me had caused my hair to fall out. I fell into a trance-like state. I was on the edge of death.

As I lay there waiting to die I heard shouting and the sensation of being dragged onto a boat. I was then transferred to a Japanese whaling vessel. I was being dropped off at a port where there were other shipwrecked POW survivors. There must have been at least one hundred of us.

We were then paraded naked through the village, apparently as some form of punishment. Some of the locals turned their backs on this demeaning procession, others jeered and spat at us. I was past caring.

And then something incredible happened. As we stumbled along in the pouring rain, someone started singing *Singin' In The Rain*. Slowly, we all joined in with altered lyrics crudely deriding our captors, unbeknownst to them. Even after all we had been through, we were defiant, our spirits unbroken.

9th August 1945 began as any other day in the POW camp; everybody had morning chores to complete before the hard labour began in the Mitsubishi factory. I was regarded as the lucky one - I tended the officers' vegetable garden.

That same morning Captain Charles Sweeney, a young US Air Force officer, aged just twenty-five, same age as myself, was beginning a day that would be anything but normal.

We didn't know that three days prior, an atomic bomb had been dropped on Hiroshima. This catastrophic bomb did not alter the Japanese hierarchy's opinion that they should fight to the death.

President Harry Truman decided that another strong message should be sent.

Sweeney's mission was to deliver an A-bomb named 'Fat Man'. At over ten feet long and five feet in diameter, it weighed in at 10,200lb.

At around midday the task I detested most was due to be done, emptying the shit-cans on to the Japanese officers' vegetables. I dry retched as usual; I just couldn't get used to that horrible stench. In its favour was the effect it had on the vegetables that were bigger and more tasty than any vege I had eaten before.

I had just completed the unpleasant task when a tremendous clap of thunder shook the very ground I was standing on. It appeared to have originated from Nagasaki city. Soon afterwards a gust of hot wind blew my one hundred-pound frame right off my feet.

Later, the other prisoners came back from their day at a nearby Mitsubishi factory and began to talk of a massive bomb raid. No one was really sure what had happened – other than it was huge.

We later learnt temperatures at ground zero were between 3,000 C and 4,000 C.

The entire area had been flattened and thirty-nine thousand Japanese had been vaporised instantly by this bomb.

**Big Boy Explodes Over Nagasaki**

**Survivors**

For several days at our camp, it was business as usual - the usual workloads, the usual beatings, and the usual meagre rations. Then on 21st August we were paraded and the Japanese commander read out the declaration of the cessation of hostilities. The war was over.

We all wondered when we would be rescued. It was time to go home.

I was working in my vegetable garden when I saw several trucks and Jeeps speed up to the camp gates. US Marines jumped out looking the epitome of American soldiers dressed in khaki, neatly pressed and waving to us as we ran towards them. They distributed cigarettes and chocolate bars. It was a frantic scene of hugs and handshakes.

Men were shouting and screaming, throwing things in the air, weeping and kissing the earth, lost in emotion. I jumped on one of the first trucks to speed out of the camp towards Nagasaki harbour, where a ship was waiting to escort us to freedom.

**Tom Doherty on the Right**

Looking out from the lorry we viewed absolute devastation, a scene from Dante's *Inferno*.

What finally dawned on me was that I had survived the most destructive bomb ever detonated. I was going home to Chesapeake Bay.'

236

# 51. The Long Road to Freedom

12th September 1942

Japanese attack Henderson again but fail, losing twelve hundred men, the Americans lose four hundred and forty six.

11th October 1942

Japanese cruisers *Furutaka* and *Fabuki* are destroyed.

13th October 1942

Japanese battleships *Kongo* and *Haruna* shell Marine positions at Henderson Field.

14th October 1942

Japanese cruisers *Chokai* and *Kinugasa* bombard the American and Allied positions.

24th–25th October 1942

Battle for Henderson Field.

26th October 1942

Battle of Santa Cruz Islands.

12th–15th November 1942

Naval battle for Guadalcanal. Japanese lose battleships *Hiei*, *Kirishishima* and the heavy cruiser *Kinguagasa*, three destroyers and seven transports.

American loses heavy cruisers *Atlanta*, *San Francisco*, light cruiser *Juneau*, and seven destroyers.

Japanese heavy cruisers *Suzuya* and *Maya* are sunk.

30th November 1942

Battle of Tassafoconga, Japan loses one destroyer, America loses heavy cruiser *North Hampton*.

9th December 1942

American PT boats sink Japanese destroyer *Teruzuki* at Cape Esperance.

15th December 1942–7th February 1943

American ground troops evict Japanese army from Guadalcanal.

29th–30th January 1943

Battle of Ronell Island. American heavy cruiser *Chicago* sunk.

1st–7th February 1943

Japanese evacuate Guadalcanal.

9th February 1943

Guadalcanal campaign is won, America and the Allies take control.

This was a significant win for America and its allies in the Pacific war. Tom's company of battle-hardened troops would take part in many more battles. Tom would have liked to be with them.

## The hard road to victory included:

10th May 1943 US Troops invade Attu in the Aleutian Islands.

14th May 1943 A Japanese submarine sinks the Australian hospital ship *Centaur* resulting in two hundred and ninety-nine dead.

31st May 1943 Japanese end their occupation of the Aleutian Islands as the US completes the capture of Attu.

21st June 1943 Allies advance to New Georgia, Solomon Islands.

8th July 1943 B-24 Liberators flying from Midway bomb Japanese on Wake Island.

6th–7th August 1943 Battle of Vella Gulf in the Solomon Islands.

25th August 1943 Allies complete the occupation of New Georgia.

4th September 1943 Allies recapture Lae-Salamaua, New Guinea.

1st November 1943 US Marines invade Bougainville in the Solomon Islands.

20th November 1943 US Troops invade Makin and Tarawa in the Gilbert Islands.

23rd November 1943 Japanese end resistance on Makin and Tarawa.

15th December 1943 US Troops land on the Arawe Peninsula of New Britain in the Solomon Islands.

26th December 1943 Full Allied assault on New Britain as 1st Division Marines invade Cape Gloucester.

9th January 1944 British and Indian troops recapture Maungdaw in Burma.

31st January 1944 US Troops invade Kwajalein in the Marshall Islands.

1st–7th February 1944 US Troops capture Kwajalein and Majura Atolls in the Marshall Islands.

17th–18th February 1944 US Carrier-based planes destroy the Japanese naval base at Truk in the Caroline Islands.

20th February 1944 US Carrier-based and land-based planes destroy the Japanese base at Rabaul.

23rd February 1944 US Carrier-based planes attack the Mariana Islands.

24th February 1944 Merrill's Marauders begin a ground campaign in northern Burma.

5th March 1944 Gen. Wingate's groups begin operations behind Japanese lines in Burma.

15th March 1944 Japanese begin offensive toward Imphal and Kohima.

17th April 1944 Japanese begin their last offensive in China, attacking US air bases in eastern China.

22nd April 1944 Allies invade Aitape and Hollandia in New Guinea.

27th May 1944 Allies invade Biak Island, New Guinea.

5th June 1944 The first mission by B-29 Superfortress bombers occurs as seventy-seven planes bomb Japanese railway facilities in Bangkok, Thailand.

15th June 1944 US Marines invade Saipan in the Mariana Islands.

15th–16th June The first bombing raid on Japan since the April 1944. Forty B-29s based in Bengal, India, target the steel works at Yawata.

19th June 1944 The 'Marianas Turkey Shoot' occurs as US Carrier-based fighters shoot down two hundred and twenty Japanese planes, while only twenty American planes are lost.

8th July 1944 Japanese withdraw from Imphal.

19th July 1944 US Marines invade Guam in the Marianas.

24th July 1944 US Marines invade Tinian.

27 July 1944 American troops complete the liberation of Guam.

3rd August 1944 US And Chinese troops take Myitkyina after a two-month siege.

8th August 1944 - American troops complete the capture of the Mariana Islands.

15th September 1944 US Troops invade Morotai and the Paulaus.

11th October 1944 US Air raids against Okinawa.

18th October 1944 Fourteen B-29s based on the Marianas attack the Japanese base at Truk.

20<sup>th</sup> October 1944 US Sixth Army invades Leyte in the Philippines.

23<sup>rd</sup>–26<sup>th</sup> October 1944 Battle of Leyte Gulf results in a decisive US Naval victory.

25<sup>th</sup> October 1944 The first suicide (*Kamikaze*) air attacks occur against US warships in Leyte Gulf. By the end of the war, Japan will have sent an estimated two thousand two hundred and fifty-seven aircraft. 'The only weapon I feared in the war,' Adm. Halsey will say later.

11<sup>th</sup> November 1944 Iwo Jima bombarded by the US Navy.

24<sup>th</sup> November Twenty-four B-29s bomb the Nakajima aircraft factory near Tokyo.

15<sup>th</sup> December 1944 US Troops invade Mindoro in the Philippines.

17<sup>th</sup> December 1944 The US Army Air Force begins preparations for dropping the Atomic Bomb by establishing the 509<sup>th</sup> Composite Group to operate the B-29s that will deliver the bomb.

3<sup>rd</sup> January 1945 Gen. MacArthur is placed in command of all US ground forces and Adm. Nimitz in command of all naval forces in preparation for planned assaults against Iwo Jima, Okinawa and Japan itself.

4<sup>th</sup> January 1945 British occupy Akyab in Burma.

9<sup>th</sup> January 1945 US Sixth Army invades Lingayen Gulf on Luzon in the Philippines.

11<sup>th</sup> January, 1945 Air raid against Japanese bases in Indochina by US Carrier-based planes.

January 28, 1945 The Burma road is reopened.

3<sup>rd</sup> February 1945 US Sixth Army attacks Japanese in Manila.

16<sup>th</sup> February 1945 US Troops recapture Bataan in the Philippines.

19<sup>th</sup> February 1945 US Marines invade Iwo Jima.

2<sup>nd</sup> March 1945 US airborne troops recapture Corregidor in the Philippines.

3rd March 1945 US And Filipino troops take Manila.

9th–10th March Fifteen square miles of Tokyo erupts in flames after it is fire bombed by two hundred and seventy-nine B-29s.

10th March 1945 US Eighth Army invades Zamboanga Peninsula on Mindanao in the Philippines.

20th March 1945 British troops liberate Mandalay, Burma.

27th March 1945 B-29s lay mines in Japan's Shimonoseki Strait to interrupt shipping.

1st April 1945 The final amphibious landing of the war occurs as the US Tenth Army invades Okinawa.

7th April 1945 B-29s fly their first fighter-escorted mission against Japan with P-51 Mustangs based on Iwo Jima; US Carrier-based fighters sink the super battleship *Yamato* and several escort vessels which planned to attack US Forces at Okinawa.

12th April 1945 President Roosevelt dies, succeeded by Harry S. Truman.

8th May 1945 Victory in Europe Day. VE.

20th May 1945 Japanese begin withdrawal from China.

25th May 1945 US Joint Chiefs of Staff approve Operation Olympic, the invasion of Japan, scheduled for November 1.

9th June 1945 Japanese Premier Suzuki announces Japan will fight to the very end rather than accept unconditional surrender.

18th June 1945 Japanese resistance ends on Mindanao in the Philippines.

22nd June 1945 Japanese resistance ends on Okinawa as the US Tenth Army completes its capture.

28th June 1945 MacArthur's headquarters announces the end of all Japanese resistance in the Philippines.

5th July 1945 Liberation of Philippines declared.

10<sup>th</sup> July 1945 1,000 bomber raids against Japan begin.

14<sup>th</sup> July 1945 The first US Naval bombardment of Japanese home islands.

16<sup>th</sup> July 1945 First atomic bomb is successfully tested in the US.

26<sup>th</sup> July 1945 Components of the atomic bomb 'Little Boy' are unloaded at Tinian Island in the South Pacific.

29<sup>th</sup> July 1945 A Japanese submarine sinks the Cruiser *Indianapolis* resulting in the loss of eight hundred and eighty-one crewmen. The ship sinks before a radio message can be sent out leaving survivors adrift for two days.

6<sup>th</sup> August 1945 First atomic bomb dropped on Hiroshima from a B-29 flown by Col. Paul Tibbets.

8<sup>th</sup> August 1945 USSR declares war on Japan then invades Manchuria.

9<sup>th</sup> August 1945 Second atomic bomb is dropped on Nagasaki from a B-29 flown by Maj. Charles Sweeney. Emperor Hirohito and Japanese Prime Minister Suzuki then decide to seek an immediate peace with the Allies.

14<sup>th</sup> August 1945 Japanese accept unconditional surrender, Gen. MacArthur is appointed to head the occupation forces in Japan.

27<sup>th</sup> August 1945 B-29s drop supplies to Allied POWs in China.

29<sup>th</sup> August 1945 The Soviets shoot down B-29 dropping supplies to POWs in Korea; US Troops land near Tokyo to begin the occupation of Japan.

30<sup>th</sup> August 1945 The British reoccupy Hong Kong.

2<sup>nd</sup> September 1945 Formal Japanese surrender ceremony on board the *Missouri* in Tokyo Bay as 1,000 carrier-based planes fly overhead. President Truman declares VJ Day.

3<sup>rd</sup> September 1945 The Japanese commander in the Philippines, Gen. Yamashita, surrenders to Gen. Wainwright at Baguio.

4<sup>th</sup> September 1945 Japanese troops on Wake Island surrender.

5<sup>th</sup> September 1945 British land in Singapore.

8<sup>th</sup> September 1945 MacArthur enters Tokyo.

9<sup>th</sup> September 1945 Japanese in Korea surrender.

13<sup>th</sup> September 1945 Japanese in Burma surrender.

**Japanese Surrender**

# 52.Free at Last

## 1$^{st}$ March 1945

Julie was completing her rounds, checking on the more serious cases amongst the women and children. The major diseases rampant within the camp were dysentery and beriberi.

Julie found it difficult being the only doctor amongst the five hundred prisoners, with very little medicine at her disposal. However, things were looking up - the Japanese had surrendered and she and the other women prisoners were waiting for the British to arrive and liberate them from their worst nightmare.

At about two in the afternoon Julie heard yells and screaming. She raced outside from the make-do hospital, concerned the Japanese had returned. She soon discovered the women were not screaming in terror but in elation: the British had arrived.

The soldiers handed out chocolate bars and cigarettes to the female prisoners and assured them that from now on they would be cared for. They were loaded on army trucks and taken to the Governor's residence where they were processed, checking their names against the lists they had, albeit they were inaccurate. The Japanese certainly didn't hand over the list of prisoners whom they had initially imprisoned. Eventually the British administration determined how many woman and children had died under Japanese rule.

In Changi alone forty percent of the women and fifty percent of the children perished under Japanese tyranny.

Julie and her daughter survived. Had Harry?

She made inquiries but nobody seemed to know. Julie asked one of her friends to look after Lara while she crossed over to the men's prison hoping she would find her husband. The men she saw were living skeletons; the Japanese had a lot to answer for. She became despondent when she couldn't find Harry anywhere. She asked fellow prisoners but got very little response. After a couple of hours she turned to leave the camp. As she walked through the gates she heard somebody calling her. Not in a voice she recognised but her name just the same. She turned and looked at the skinny, gaunt man. Julie didn't recognise him until he looked at her with those beautiful blue eyes. They were sunken, but that blue - it was Harry, he was alive. They both walked as fast as their emaciated frames could take them and just hugged, they couldn't let go.

The family had survived.


Jack had been posted in London for most of the war. Although he had held important intelligence positions he had no way of discovering whether his son Tom had survived the Pacific war. He knew that Peter had received serious wounds and was sent home. Now that peace had been declared he hoped he would find out the information he knew would bring him either elation or grief.

**VE Day Celebrations**

**VP Day Celebrations**

Jack had been in constant contact with Macarthur's office since the Japanese surrender, but they had not been able to establish if Tom was in Singapore or had been shipped elsewhere.

# 2<sup>nd</sup> March 1945

Jack was in his office finalising his reports and preparing to fly back to Washington. Lucy was responsible for supervising the removalists. Jack was sure they had twice as many goods and chattels than when they arrived.

The phone rang and a weak voice at the end of the line said, 'Hello Dad'.

'Tom? Tom! Is that you?'

'Yep! It's me.'

'Thank God! I've been so worried. Where are you?'

'On the *Saratoga*. Heading back to San Diego.'

'I'm flying out with your Mother in a couple of days. We can meet you there.'

'That'd be great, Dad. Can't talk any longer. There's a queue of Marines waiting to make their calls.'

'OK son. Oh thank God, you're alive. You're alive! Now I know where you are I can get in touch.'

'Yeah, I figured a Two-Star general would be able to swing a call.'

'Three-Star now, Tom. But who's counting. We can talk about that when we see you.'

Jack put the telephone down and started to sob; he couldn't stop. His secretary knocked and entered. She couldn't understand why the General was weeping. He gained some composure and explained the situation. She too became emotional and went around the desk and hugged the man she had always admired for his toughness. Jack decided to leave the office and tell Lucy face to face. Needless to say it was an evening of joy yet tears - their Tommy was alive.

One outstanding issue was the whereabouts and welfare of his sister Julie and her husband Harry, as well as his grand-niece Lara. He knew they had been caught up in the Japanese invasion of Singapore but nothing else. Information was beginning to filter through about the atrocious conditions and cruelty meted out by the Japanese in Changi and other prisons in Singapore. He could only pray that they had survived. Two weeks later he learnt that they had and were on their way back to England by ship.

Jack was the patriarch of the Doherty family. He was delighted that despite terrible conditions his two sons, his sister and his grand-niece had all survived a terrible war.

**The Price They Pay**

# 53. Family Reunion

## London March 1946

The day arrived when Jack and Anna boarded the Lockheed Constellation bound for New York City. From there they would fly to Washington where Jack would officially hand over his papers to his superior, the Secretary of the Navy, James Forrestal. His mother's husband, Gene Leutze was Forrestal's predecessor but had died from a heart attack in 1944. He didn't live to see the end of the war.

After the normal procedures were completed Jack and Lucy flew to Los Angeles and then on to San Diego to meet with their son Tom.

Tom was waiting for them at the airport. The marine commander at the base had organised a car to take him there and wherever else he desired to go with his parents.

Jack and Lucy walked across the tarmac in great anticipation - they hadn't seen their son for over four years. Once inside the terminal they eagerly looked around to see if they could find him. He was standing right in front of them, a skinny, gaunt figure of a man in a marine captain's uniform that was way too large for him.

'Hi Mom. Hi Dad. Don't you recognise me in uniform?' he said with a broad smile on his face.

'Tom, my darling boy! What have they done to you?' his mother cried.

'Hi Dad. Should I salute the three-star General or give you a hug?'

'Oh son! A hug would be just fine, Captain.'

They hugged each other like never before; tears were flowing from all three.

'You must tell us all you've been through Tommy,' Lucy said through tears.

'Not now Mom. Not everything. I don't want to relive some of the experiences. Let's get your bags and we can get out of here. I've booked a fantastic restaurant on the beach we can talk there.'

The three Doherty family members enjoyed their lunch of lobster and finished with Tom's favourite desert, apple pie and ice cream. A far cry from the cup of rice he was allocated each day while in captivity. Jack told Tom about his brother's experience during and after the D-Day landings and how he had been seriously wounded. Tom was looking forward to seeing his brother when he visited Washington.

One story Tom did share was surviving the atomic bomb in Nagasaki; both parents were flabbergasted.

Jack and Lucy were required back in Washington the next day but made a pact with Tom that he and the rest of the clan meet at the Chesapeake holiday home the following July.

Tom was due back at the base by 5 pm so they said their goodbyes at the restaurant.

# Britain 1946

Harry and Julie departed for Southampton on 4th March approximately six months after they were liberated. It had taken this amount of time for Harry to gain weight and strength to embark on such a long journey.

They arrived in their beloved England on 6th May. The sea journey seemed like it would never end for the pair, however Lara loved it, playing with the young friends she had met on the RMS *Queen Elizabeth*.

A car had been arranged by the caretaker of Westmoreland Manor, Mr Bryant, to pick them up from the wharf and transport them home to their London residence.

As the car pulled into the long paved driveway lined with English oak trees Harry and Julie breathed a sigh of relief - they were home. Lara was in awe.

'Imagine playing in these gardens,' she thought.

This was to be a journey of rediscovery. Mr Bryant took their luggage to the master bedroom and Lara's to the suite opposite.

The next few weeks entailed catching up with old friends and sadly learning that some had died in the war.

Deciding that Harry needed a rest from all the social activities, Julie arranged for the family to travel up to County Durham and stay at Raby Castle for a month or so. Harry certainly didn't argue; he loved the castle and all the wildlife and was looking forward to some shooting.

The month passed quickly and soon the family was due to return to London so that Lara could begin school. Harry and Julie had discussed their careers at length and both decided that private practice specialising in plastic surgery would best suit them. They established a surgery in Harley Street, London and started seeing patients in June 1947. Initially the majority of their patients sustained facial injuries as a result of 'The Blitz.'

# 54. Three Hour Cruise

**The *Intrepid***

## July 1948

Jack and Anna had been planning the family holiday at Chesapeake since war's end when they discovered the entire family had survived the horrors of the shocking conflict in Europe and the Pacific.

Julie and Harry were taking time off from their medical practice in London and flying to New York then on to Washington. From there they would meet Tom and Peter and drive to Chesapeake. They decided to leave Lara with her nanny, as they felt the trip would be too arduous.

Lucy, the matriarch of the family was now seventy-one yet quite active, and had been living at the Chesapeake beach house since the death of her husband Gene.

On 3rd July the family all arrived at the house. It was first time in years that the clan had got together for a holiday.

At six that evening the dinner bell was rung by Anna, summoning everybody to meet in the summer room overlooking the bay. She asked Peter to pop the corks on two bottles of 1928 vintage Krug. Joe, her first husband had been storing it in the wine cellar below the house for many years.

'I would like everybody to charge their glasses. Here's to the Doherty family - long may we live.'

'Hear, hear!' they all responded.

'Mother, this champagne is magnificent! Where on earth did you find it?' asked Tom.

'My little secret, darling, But I can tell you there's more where that came from.'

Jack rose and proposed another toast.

'Here's to my father Joe and to my stepfather Gene. May they both rest in peace.'

'Thank you, darling,' his mother smiled.

After the toasts were over they moved into the dining room where Sarah the maid had set a beautiful table.

The meal was wonderful, incorporating seafood and roast loin of lamb. The wine was Californian.

'Well everybody, it wasn't too long ago that I was sitting in the dust with my bowl and a handful of rice. When I was marched through the gates of River Valley Road Camp my weight was one hundred and eighty pounds. When I was liberated, I was down to ninety pounds. And now here I am with the people I love most in the world eating fine food and drinking excellent wine. I thank God I am alive. By the way I now weigh one hundred and seventy pounds.' Tom's eyes welled with tears.

'A toast to Tom.' Lucy held her up glass and everybody followed her lead.

'Unfortunately, Julie and I can tell a very similar story to Tom's. All we would like to say is we are very happy to be with you all - alive,' Harry said.

'May I suggest we retire into the lounge room. I have another surprise for you all.'

The family did as requested, and found waiting for them were brandy balloons and a very impressive bottle of cognac.

'This bottle of cognac has been in our cellar for as long as I remember, unopened. It is Louis XIII. I quote,

'It's one century in a glass,' Louis XIII's cellar master Pierrette Trichet said, holding a crystal glass filled with amber liquid. 'The idea is to be very humble in front of this glass and pay respect because it represents the effort and the know-how of one century.'

'Peter, may I ask you to pour a glass for each of us please?'

'Certainly, Mother.'

'Tomorrow I have arranged to take the launch out on the bay. We will enjoy our 4th of July lunch cruising. I have asked Joe Wilcox to act as skipper so we can enjoy ourselves without worrying about steering the boat as it were.'

Gradually the family retired to their bedrooms except Peter and Tom.

'How are your legs holding up Pete?'

'Yeah, they're OK. I get pain when it gets cold.'

'You'd better move to California then.'

'That's not such a bad idea, Tom. Actually, I'm seriously thinking of doing just that.'

'Really?'

'Yeah, I'm thinking of leaving the Marines and enrolling at Stanford. I want to do a post-grad in neurosurgery.'

'Wow, that's a big one. Why neurosurgery?'

'I saw so many head wounds in the war. I felt helpless not being able to help the poor bastards. I also look at Julie and Harry and the fantastic work they're doing changing people's lives. I'd like to make a similar contribution.'

'Good on you Pete. That's great.'

'So how goes it with you, Tom?'

'It's been hard. Real hard. I suffered like you wouldn't believe under the Japs. When I was fighting, it all seemed worthwhile. You were doing something for your pals and your country. Once captured you felt worthless. A failure somehow.'

Tom opened up and recounted the hell ships and his survival of the A-bomb at Nagasaki.

Peter was aghast.

'I knew it must have been hell, but I had no idea.'

'Yeah! It was fucking horrible. Don't tell Mom. It would distress her too much.'

'Sure.'

They hugged each other and retired for the night.

# 4<sup>th</sup> July 1948

The Dohertys had breakfast together in the summer room: pancakes with strawberries, blueberries and vanilla ice cream; red white and blue.

The men each took a basket of wine while the women carried the food, which was to be the Independence Day lunch.

Once they had boarded, the skipper asked the Doherty men to cast off the ropes and they were underway. The weather was perfect; blue skies with the odd puffy white cloud. The only fault was that the wind had picked up and was quite strong. This was of no concern to the *Intrepid* - she was one hundred feet long and powered by an eight hundred horsepower diesel engine.

About an hour out from the shore the women started to prepare the lunch in the galley while the men were on deck talking, smoking and generally enjoying themselves.

At 1 pm Julie called the boys down to have their lunch. Harry had just lit a large Cuban cigar and was annoyed that he had to throw it over the side; however he did as he was told. The group, including Joe the skipper, were seated at the yacht's dining table and before them were various dishes, all decorated with the stars and stripes.

> 'Well, just eighteen months ago who would have thought this could possibly happen?, Sitting down to a fabulous fourth of July lunch on a luxury yacht in the middle of Chesapeake Bay,' Tom said.
>
> 'I agree Tom. We've all very lucky considering what we've all been through,' agreed Pete.
>
> 'I smell smoke. Can anybody else smell it?' asked Julie.
>
> 'It's probably the smoke from Harry's cigar still lingering about,' said Pete. 'Bloody cigars! They'll kill you one day Harry.'
>
> 'No, it's not cigar smoke. I quite like the smell of a fine cigar.' there was an edge of concern in Julie's voice.
>
> 'The hot plates aren't on are they Mum?'

'No. I haven't used them today. We cooked up at the house.'

'Look! There's smoke coming in under the galley door. There must be a fire up on deck!' Joe was panicked.

'You ladies stay down here. We'll check out what's happening,' instructed Pete.

'Shit! The doors locked. No that's impossible. Must be jammed.'

The four men tried to push the door open but it wouldn't budge. They grabbed the fire extinguisher and began bashing the door with the heavy cylinder. Not what it was designed for in the case of a fire. The galley was filling with smoke causing everybody to start coughing uncontrollably. They tried bashing the portholes with the fire extinguisher but it made no impact. Harry told the women to lie on the floor below the smoke cloud although that seemed to make no difference. The heat emanating from the fire became intense, singing the hairs on the men's arms.

What Harry or any of the others hadn't realised was that the cigar had blown back onto the rear deck. It had landed on a loosely coiled rope and began to smoulder. The wind and the cruiser's movement fanned the small fire. Within a few minutes it had become a major outbreak. Unfortunately the blaze was located over the reserve fuel tank and set off an explosion that could be heard miles away. *Intrepid* burned furiously and within thirty minutes was a smouldering wreck barely above the waterline.

All on board perished.

The Dohertys had survived the war, the POW camps and the *Titanic*. Now they were all gone, except for Lara.

# The End

# Bibliography

List of people associated with Bletchley Park, Wikipedia, the free encyclopedia
http://en.wikipedia.org/wiki/List_of_people_associated_with_Bletchley_Park
Bletchley Park gets personal with new Alan Turing exhibition The Register
www.theregister.co.uk/2012/03/06/new_turing_exhibition_bletchley_park/
Operation Fortitude- Wikipedia, the free encyclopedia
http://en.wikipedia.org/wiki/Operation_Fortitude
The Leaders of D-Day http://www.military.com/forums/0,15240,137800,00.html
The British Army's fight against Venereal Disease in the 'Heroic Age of
Prostitution' http://ww1centenary.oucs.ox.ac.uk/body-and-mind/the-british-
army%E2%80%99s-fight-against-venereal-disease-in-the-%E2%80%98heroic-
age-of-prostitution%E2%80%99/
The Yalta Conference (1945)
http://www.thelatinlibrary.com/imperialism/notes/yalta.html
List of World War II conferences - Wikipedia, the free encyclopedia
http://en.wikipedia.org/wiki/List_of_World_War_II_conferences
World War II Memo Cracked by Allies Found -History in the Headlines
http://www.history.com/news/world-war-ii-memo-cracked-by-allies-found
The Anzac landing at Gallipoli - Reports by war correspondents Gallipoli and
the Anzacs http://www.anzacsite.gov.au/1landing/bartlett.html
BBC News – Why border lines drawn with a ruler In WW1still rock the Middle
East http://www.bbc.com/news/world-middle-east-25299553
Operation Fortitude - Wikipedia, the free encyclopedia
Operation Fortitude
https://www.princeton.edu/~achaney/tmve/wiki100k/docs/Operation_Fortitude.h
tml
Operation Fortitude http://www.dday-overlord.com/eng/operation_fortitude.htm
D-Day Fact Sheet http://www.kansasheritage.org/abilene/ikedday.html
WWII Statistics http://www.angelfire.com/ct/ww2europe/stats.html
Attack on Pearl Harbor- Wikipedia, the free encyclopedia
http://en.wikipedia.org/wiki/Attack_on_Pearl_Harbor
How the U.S. Cracked Japan's 'Purple Encryption Machine' at the Dawn of
World War II http://www.intelligence-world.org/how-the-u-s-cracked-japans-
purple-encryption-machine-at-the-dawn-of-world-war-ii/
Guadalcanal Campaign, August 1942 - February 1943
http://www.history.navy.mil/photos/events/wwii-pac/guadlcnl/guadlcnl.htm
Guadalcanal Campaign - Wikipedia, the free encyclopedia
http://en.wikipedia.org/wiki/Guadalcanal_Campaign
Blog Archive • The Land Campaign for Guadalcanal August1942 - February
1943 http://blog.usni.org/2009/10/16/the-land-campaign-for-guadalcanal-august-
1942-february-1943
The History Place - Timeline of Pacific War
http://www.historyplace.com/unitedstates/pacificwar/timeline.htm
The Alexandra Massacre http://en.wikipedia.org/wiki/Alexandra_Hospital
Australians at War http://www.australiansatwar.gov.au/

After the shooting, PoWs found redemption in sport The Australian
http://www.theaustralian.com.au/arts/review/after-the-shooting-pows-found-redemption-in-sport/story-fn9n8gph-1226303915162
1948 Chris -Craft 18 Sportsman Utility- Boats.com http://www.boats.com/boat-details/Chris-Craft-18-Sportsman-Utility/144364241#.VFHTNfmUd8E
1948 Matthews 40' Sedan Cruiser Classic Yacht – Home http://www.matthewsboat.us/
Gordon Bennett http://www.fepow-community.org.uk/monthly_revue/html/gordon_bennett.htm
Changi – The beginnings of Changi http://www.abc.net.au/changi/history/
Changi Australian War Memorial
http://www.awm.gov.au/encyclopedia/pow/changi/
Nagasaki saved my life: How one PoW survived Burma's death railway, Japanese hell ships AND the atom bomb
http://www.dailymail.co.uk/news/article-1254453/Nagasaki-saved-life-How-PoW-survived-Burmas-death-railway-Japanese-hellships-AND-atom-bomb.html
HyperWar: U.S. Naval Admin in WW II: The U.S. Navy Medical Dept at War,1941-194S Chapter 171 http://ibiblio.org/hyperwar/USN/Admin-Hist/USN-Admin/index.html
BBC- WW2 People's War - D-Day+ 1944 Category
http://www.bbc.co.uk/history/ww2peopleswar/categories/c54665/
History News Network Hitler's Carmaker: The Inside Story of How General Motors Helped Mobilize the Third Reich (Part 1)
http://www.globalresearch.ca/hitler-s-carmaker-the-inside-story-of-how-general-motors-helped-mobilize-the-third-reich/5571
Military Intelligence Quotes
http://www.brainyquote.com/quotes/keywords/military_intelligence.html
Georgetown University – The James D. Mooney Papers: Collection Description
http://www.library.georgetown.edu/dept/speccoll/cl98.htm
Henry Ford, the Nazi Party and evil – traitor to the US
http://www.clarkstonnews.com/Articles-i-2011-01-05-239451.113121-sub-Henry-Ford-the-Nazi-Party-and-eviltraitor-to-the-US.html
Ford's Anti-Semitism: Henry Ford. WGBH American Experience IPBS
http://www.pbs.org/wgbh/americanexperience/features/interview/henryford-antisemitism/
MHC RELATIONS WITH JAPAN 1938-1940
https://www.mtholyoke.edu/acad/intrel/WorldWar2/japan.htm
Sarajevo, June 28, 1914 http://net.lib.byu.edu/estu/wwi/comment/sarajevo.html
History of Singapore - Wikipedia, the free encyclopedia
http://en.wikipedia.org/wiki/History_of_Singapore
Living in distrust and constant fear
http://ourstory.asia1.com.sg/war/headline/torture2.html
How Did The British Govern Singapore Before WWI
http://www.slideshare.net/missfateha/sec-2-history-chapter-5
Imperialism In Singapore- Daily Life Under Imperial Rule
http://singaporelife.tumblr.com/post/426369826/daily-life-under-imperial-rule

Battle of Singapore Wikipedia, the free encyclopedia
http://en.wikipedia.org/wiki/Battle_of_Singapore
Alistair Urquhart – Wikipedia, the free encyclopedia
http://en.wikipedia.org/wiki/Alistair_Urquhart
South African artist to honour 'lost men' of WWI
http://www.southafrica.info/about/arts/art-151113.htm#.VFMAd_mUd8E
4th December 1941: The British reinforce Singapore http://ww2today.com/4th-december-1941-the-british-reinforce-singapore
13th February 1942: Desperate last hours in Singapore
http://ww2today.com/13th-february-1942-desperate-last-hours-in-singapore
The fall of Singapore
http://www.historylearningsite.co.uk/fall_of_singapore.htm
Battle of Singapore – Wikipedia, the free encyclopedia
http://en.wikipedia.org/wiki/Battle_of_Singapore
Singapore Defences http://www.britain-at-war.org.uk/WW2/Malaya_and_Singapore/html/singapore_defences.htm
Charles Joseph Pemberton Paglar infopedia
http://eresources.nlb.gov.sg/infopedia/articles/SIP_1228_2008-11-28.html
Invasion of Malaya and Singapore, World War II Database
http://ww2db.com/battle_spec.php?battle_id=47
1940 WW2 Events Time Line http://www.secondworldwarhistory.com/1940-ww2-events-timeline.asp
Sink the Bismarck Timeline1941 http://www.secondworldwarhistory.com/sink-the-bismarck.asp
Enigma coding machine used by Nazis in WWII to be sold at auction
http://www.dailymail.co.uk/news/article-2038491/Enigma-coding-machine-used-Nazis-WWII-sold-auction.html
Bletchley Park – Wikipedia, the free encyclopedia
http://en.wikipedia.org/wiki/Bletchley_Park
Enigma Machine http://www.bbc.co.uk/history/topics/enigma ,
Women Codebreakers – Bletchley Park Research
http://www.bletchleyparkresearch.co.uk/research-notes/women-codebreakers/
Alan Turing Scrapbook – The Enigma War
http://www.turing.org.uk/scrapbook/ww2.html
thelen.org/comp-hist/NSA-Enigma http://ed-thelen.org/comp-hist/NSA-Enigma.html
History News Network, Hitler's Carmaker: The Inside Story of How General Motors Helped Mobilize the Third Reich (Part I)
http://historynewsnetwork.org/article/37935
Georgetown University – The James D. Mooney Papers: Collection Description
http://www.library.georgetown.edu/dept/speccoll/fl/f98%7d1.htm

# Copyright

ISBN: 9781925280050 (p/b)
ISBN: 9781925280067 (eBook)

Survival is a work of fiction.. Any resemblance to real persons, living or dead, is purely coincidental.